S.I.P.

Cassie
Binegar

Cassie
Binegar

Patricia MacLachlan

A HARPER TROPHY BOOK

HARPER & ROW, PUBLISHERS

The portion of the poem "Old Old Woman, Little Girl" by Brendan Galvin that appears on page 1 is reprinted from *Atlantic Flyway* by permission of The University of Georgia Press. © 1980 by The University of Georgia Press.

Cassie Binegar
Copyright © 1982 by Patricia MacLachlan
First Harper Trophy edition, 1987

Library of Congress Cataloging in Publication Data
MacLachlan, Patricia.
  Cassie Binegar.

  "A Charlotte Zolotow book."
  Summary: During the summer Cassie learns to accept
change and to find her own space.
  [1. Family life—Fiction] I. Title.
PZ7.M2225Cas 1982   [Fic]   81-48641
ISBN 0-06-024033-4   AACR2
ISBN 0-06-024034-2 (lib. bdg.)

  "A Harper Trophy book"
ISBN 0-06-440195-2 (pbk.)

For Ann, Dale, and Shulamith
—companions throughout the process—

Contents

Contents

One is beginning to learn
What the other is forgetting,
One preparing to go
Where the other has been,
And they feed each other
From kitchen chairs,
The space between
As clear as a sky beyond

Two branches, one tapering out,
The second, a nub of everything possible. . . .

Brendan Galvin
"Old Old Woman, Little Girl"
Atlantic Flyway

1

Infinity

CASSIE BINEGAR (whose name rhymes with vinegar) sat on a sand dune by the sea, being angry. I AM ANGRY, she wrote in big letters in the sand. "What's written becomes truth," her fourth-grade teacher had once said, and Cassie believed him. She carried a lined-white-paper list of complaints and angers, now numbering twenty-two and ranging from too many relatives to dry skin to this lonely place where she now lived. Cassie sighed and smoothed over the letters with a sweep of her hand and wrote I AM INFINITELY ANGRY.

3

Cassie liked the word infinity. It was a big word with a big meaning. It was an i-n-f-i-n-i-t-e word.

A sea wind came up, and a tiny land crab walked sideways through the tail of the Y in INFINITELY. Cassie frowned and watched the sea. The sand and water stretched out as far as she could see. The spring sky, the color blue of her mother's garden irises, was huge and cloudless. There were no neat fenced-in yards or sidewalks or boundaries in this new place. After one sand dune, there was another. After one wave, another came behind. Even the birds moved endlessly, the gulls wheeling above, the sanderlings darting before the waves below, always running just out of the way of the white curls of water. Cassie had tried running from the waves herself, but she was almost always caught by the water, sometimes in her good shoes.

The thought of shoes made Cassie frown again, for shoes had been one of the reasons they had moved to this lonely place.

"Can't afford to shoe the family," she had heard her father complain. "Boots for James, growing like sourweed. Boots and foul-weather gear for John Thomas. School shoes for Cassie." And her parents had moved here to Snow Shore from their house inland. It was closer to her father and brothers' fishing boat, and her mother could tend and

4

rent the cottages that spread about the house like seeds sown from an apron.

Cassie turned her back on the sea and looked up at the new house. *New* house! It was old and gray and weathered, with only one scrub pine in the side yard—a tree so wind-wild and stunted that it didn't even reach the roof. The garden was scattered, a clump of irises here, a nest of nasturtiums there, and beach plums and sea roses everywhere.

Cassie thought longingly of the order and pattern in her mother's old garden inland. And her old tree house, built on the low limbs of a huge maple tree. It had been her space. Here there was no space for her. Even her own room was not hers. There was faded wallpaper—cabbage roses, her mother said—hung there by those who had lived there before. And there were worn places on the wooden floors that someone else had patterned.

In the beginning, when they had first come, the old attic had been Cassie's space. There was a small round window there, and if Cassie lay on her stomach she could see the water, the sand, and the winding sea roads. She had arranged her books there—her dictionary, her thesaurus, and her notebooks—hidden from the rest of her family. She began her poem "Spaces" there.

> *Except for tops that spin*
>   *And books and poems*
>   *And my father's grin,*
> *I like spaces best of all.*
> *Inside, outside, upsidedownside,*
> *Narrow spaces where I can crawl.*

She had searched through her dictionary for words to describe the new house. She had found three so far, all D words: dreary, depressing, decadent. She had become strangely content in her attic space. But soon, piece by piece, furniture and trunks and old suitcases tied with string took over the attic, moving her out.

Then Cassie found a door hidden under the back stairway, with a bare hanging light inside. She spent hours there, reading and writing.

> *Inside my house*
>   *Under a chair,*
>   *Behind a door*
>   *In my lion's lair;*
> *Pausing, whisperlike, on a stair,*
> *I listen, hear, and stop to see,*
> *And no one ever knows it's me.*

>   *"Hush," says my mother. "Is that a mouse?"*
>   *When it's only me, hiding in my house.*

But before Cassie could make this space her own, her older brothers and her father began to use it for their boots and fishing gear. Then the smell of the sea invaded and swept her away.

"Come out, come out, wherever you are," called her laughing brothers, allowing her no privacy. And they pulled her into the kitchen, where they would spin another tale of a fish lost.

"Good!" Cassie would cry adamantly, her heart with the escaped fish.

"Another one for Cass," her father would say, reaching over to take her hand. "Another Big Jim"—his name for every big fish that got away.

Cassie moved into each cottage then, one by one, taking her pen and notebook and books. The cottages were private and scattered, some hidden between grassy dunes, one high on a bluff so that Cassie could watch for the intruders that were her family. But slowly, her mother came behind her to scrape and paint and put up new curtains. "To get ready for the summer people next year," she said.

"But I need a space!" cried Cassie. "A space of my own."

Her mother, tall and lean and out of sorts, took her outside and waved her arm. "Cass, there's space here. Space for everyone!"

But Cassie shook her head. It's not *my* space, she thought.

Her new friend Margaret Mary lived in a shiny house that had lots of spaces for Margaret Mary.

Cassie had visited her and seen that at least *she* fit in her family. She had neat braids and matching dresses and socks. She had a very neat dollhouse, neatly arranged, with matching sets of furniture. Even the doll's toilet was in the doll's bathroom. Cassie thought about her own secondhand dollhouse, passed down to her from now-old cousins, with its tumble of new and used furniture, just like Cassie's house.

Margaret Mary's mother was a proper mother, too. She did not wear her husband's work shirts as Cassie's mother did, or knit too-big sweaters and laugh at the mistakes and leave them in the sweater! Margaret Mary's mother wore high-heeled shoes that made sharp clicking noises when she walked. You could always tell where she was and where she was going just by listening. She even had her canned goods in alphabetical order: artichoke hearts, broccoli, corn.

Margaret Mary's father wore a neat suit and carried a black briefcase and came home at five-thirty every evening to give whoever stood by the front door a tidy kiss. Cassie's father and brothers came home with the tides, smelling of fish, and they'd whirl her up in their arms and touch her hello with rough, rope-worn hands.

"Am I adopted?" asked Cassie after visiting Margaret Mary's house for the first time.

"Adopted!" Her mother laughed, pushing her

8

long curly hair back with both hands. "We would have adopted you if we had known you. We've told you where you were born."

"We never made it to the hospital with you," her father said, his voice soft. "You were born in a taxi."

"A taxi!" exclaimed Cassie. She told them about Margaret Mary, born in a city hospital with soft lights, hushed voices, and her father swooping ("swooping" was Margaret Mary's word) into the room with an armful of roses.

"No roses," said Cassie's mother, putting her hand on her husband's arm. "But your father raced through the crowd and bought a bunch of violets from a lady on the street corner."

"Why didn't he send the taxi driver?" grumped Cassie.

"Because the taxi driver was helping," said her mother.

"Helping!" shrieked Cassie. "A stranger?"

"He's not a stranger," said her mother firmly. "We hear from him every year at Christmas."

"If it's swooping you want," said her oldest brother John Thomas, "then swooping is what you'll get." And he whirled Cassie up in his arms, swinging her up and down and around. "Swoop!" he called. "Swoop, swoop, we are swooping your new baby to you, Madam."

Cassie, furious, couldn't help laughing as John

Thomas deposited her in her mother's lap.

"Lovely child," announced James, smiling and peering at her. "But bald, I'm sad to tell. She looks like a soccer ball."

"Don't all babies?" asked John Thomas.

Alone on the dune staring at the house, Cassie touched her cheek. She could almost feel her mother's coarse curly hair against her face, John Thomas's rough hand holding hers, see the look of her father's face, softened by the glow of the oil lamp, and James' wide smile, his eyes crinkled by early crow's-feet. A sudden breaking of the gulls overhead made Cassie look up. The gulls were like her family, noisy and raucous. There was always laughing and kissing and bumping and touching. Cassie winced, hunching her shoulders in protection against the thoughts of their loud love. She thought enviously of Margaret Mary's mother, who looked serene. Cassie had practiced looking serene each morning before breakfast.

"What's the trouble, Cass?" her mother had asked. "A headache?" She had brushed Cassie's hair off her forehead and put her lips there. "A fever?"

Cassie shook her head, thinking of it. A great cloud—where had it come from?—slid over the sun, and Cassie shivered. Her mother came out of the house and called to her.

"Cass, time to set the table!"

Cassie stood up, watching the wind lift her mother's long hair and push it in front of her face.

Sudden anger pushed at the back of Cassie's throat.

"No," she shouted suddenly. "I'm upset and angry. I don't want to set the table. I don't like it here. And I don't like you much, either!"

But the wind, as Cassie had known it would, tossed the words back into her mouth. Her mother, not hearing, held out her arms and beckoned her home.

Cassie took out her lined-white-paper list, and while her mother waited she wrote one more complaint:

23. TOO MUCH INFINITY.

Then she sighed and slowly walked up the hill.

2

Day Dreams, Night Dreams

THE OLD MEMORY began again, even before dinner was over. Usually it came to Cassie as a dream, most often at night. But lately it came during the day, invading the safety of daylight. Cassie had made the dream go away before by pressing her fingers against her eyelids, tightly, so that waves and flashes came instead. But it didn't work anymore. And today it was her mother's fault. Right in the middle of dinner, in the midst of her brothers' teasing, her father's laughter, Cassie's mother made the announcement.

"Gran's coming for a while."

12

Suddenly, for Cassie, all the noises stopped. She pushed her plate away and watched her father's lips move.

"That's good," he said, looking up, his fork poised. "It will be good for her. She can help get the cottages ready."

"The others would like to come, too," added her mother. "They can all help. All right?" She bent her head to include the family in the decision.

"You mean Uncle Hat?" asked John Thomas, smiling broadly. "And Cousin Coralinda?"

"And Baby Binnie?" James began laughing. They all laughed. All but Cassie. The picture of her grandfather, Papa, lying in the big oak bed in the old house inland, came between Cassie and her family. And the memory came, washing over her like a sea wave.

"Come, come, Cassie," Papa was saying as if it were yesterday. "Moving to the sea will be an adventure. There will be sand, miles of it, and the ocean and birds! And in the summers there will be people to rent the cottages. New people for you to know. Maybe new people each summer." He held out his thin arms to hug her, but Cassie, as in every memory, as in every dream, shrugged him away. "No!" she said, stamping her foot stubbornly. "I don't want to leave here. Something terrible will happen if we move. You'll see. You'll see!"

And soon after, something terrible *had* happened. Papa had died.

"Say you're sorry for yelling," Papa had called after her. "Say you're sorry."

But Cassie had run off.

"We can put them all up in the cottages," came her mother's voice. "As long as it stays this warm."

I'm sorry, I'm sorry, thought Cassie. But as often as she tried to change the words, she had not said she was sorry. Would things have been different if she had? She had not gone to Papa's funeral. She had stayed with a friend and watched out the window as the long line of cars passed by on their way to bury her grandfather. Seventeen. She had counted them as her friend played solitaire in the room.

"Twenty-five, thirty-five, forty," said her friend, counting points to a game.

"Seventeen cars," Cassie had answered her, her nose pressed against the window.

"Seventeen what?" asked James, nudging Cassie from her dream. And it was now again. Her Gran coming. Coming to stay. She would see, and Cassie would not be able to hide anymore.

"Seventeen nothing," said Cassie, trying to smile at James.

Dinner was over, and Cassie's mother was taking out her flute to play.

"Mom?" pleaded Cassie suddenly.

"Mom what?" asked her mother. She played a quick scale, a fluid sound like water calling down the side of a hill.

"Nothing," said Cassie, the words she wanted to say gone the way of the music. "Nothing."

She slipped out of her chair, taking her plate and her mother's, and went to lean against the kitchen sink. The sweet sad sound of her mother's flute made her throat tighten.

She had not seen Gran alone since the funeral, afraid that Gran, so good at seeing the truths behind Cassie's words, might see the truth about Cassie. She had yelled at Papa. She was ashamed of her family. She wished for things to be different. No, she wished for things to be the same, the way they had been. Gran was coming, and she would see.

Cassie looked up and stared at the dark window over the sink.

"What do you see?" asked James, putting his arm around Cassie's shoulders.

Cassie saw herself looking back, large eyed and wavery, like a ghost.

"Me," said Cassie.

"Only you?" asked James. "There's a moon on the water, can't you see? And a boat out there. Look, she's got her running lights on." He bent down, his head next to Cassie's, and pointed. Cassie closed her eyes and opened them again. She shook her head and tried to look beyond the staring face in the window glass. Behind them, Cassie's mother began playing a quick piece, and Cassie could see her reflection get up and begin to dance and weave around the room in time to the music. Cassie could see her wiggle and hear John Thomas and her father laugh.

Cassie sighed.

"Why can't we be like everyone else?" she asked.

James looked down at her.

"And what is everyone else like, Cass?" he asked softly. He folded his arms, waiting. But there was no answer.

"You don't understand," said Cassie, angrily.

You don't understand. Cassie thought of Margaret Mary and her family who wore shoes most times and had matching silverware. Margaret Mary liked Cassie. But now it would be ruined. Cassie's relatives, Cassie thought, were even worse than her family. They would spoil everything. Uncle Hat, who often talked in numbers and rhymes. His daughter, Cousin Coralinda, who wore too many feathers, with her baby, Binnie. And worst of all, Gran, with her sharp eyes, quick, darting, like the sandpipers, and her blunt words.

Sighing, Cassie tried once more to look beyond

16

the face in the glass. There was the sea out there, now black in the darkness, and a moon, and the every-so-often sweep of the Coast Guard light. But Cassie couldn't see them. James was right. Her own face was in the way.

3

Inside, Outside

IN THE BEGINNING, Margaret Mary and Cassie had been careful friends, circling each other, making uneasy, measured reachings of friendship like dogs meeting for the first time. *I know you're a dog. I am, too. Sniff a bit. Will I like you? More important, will you like me?* In school, where Cassie had come during the mid-year, there were others her age, all accepting, none unfriendly. But there was something about Margaret Mary, newly arrived from England. Something special in the mysterious prim set of her mouth that twitched up in a smile at odd times, the clipped way of speaking. Some-

18

thing special like a secret signal or a whisper or a flower suddenly blooming between two rocks. Margaret Mary was a comfortable mystery to Cassie. She listened to Cassie complain about her family, her house, her need for a space, her wish to go back. She listened and said little. And as Cassie drew comfort from Margaret Mary's accepting silence, she basked in the order of Margaret Mary's house. The tables were not cluttered with books and magazines. They were bare and shiny and you could not write messages in the dust. Margaret Mary's mother and father discussed the morning newspaper and the evening news in soft voices that did not rise or fall with annoying enthusiasm. The conversation wafted above Cassie and Margaret Mary's heads like steam from hot tea. Margaret Mary's mother and father did not ask Cassie any embarrassing questions about what she thought and how she felt about things. They only asked her where she lived and if she had brothers and sisters and what her parents did for a living. Then she was left to think, and eat off the matching white plates with gold rims, dishes that were whisked away and put in a dishwasher. Cassie saw that the kitchen counters were shiny and unstained. The faucet did not drip. And there were no ants.

In Margaret Mary's bedroom there was a place for everything and the bed was so neat that Cassie wondered if Margaret Mary actually slept in it.

"Your parents are nice," said Cassie, suddenly shy.

Margaret Mary looked up, one eyebrow raised. "Yes," she said thoughtfully. "They are nice."

"Your house is nice, too," said Cassie, sitting on the bed. "And your room," she added. Cassie stood up. "Where's the bathroom?"

Margaret Mary smiled and pointed.

"It's there," she said, grinning. "It's nice, too."

Cassie grinned back at Margaret Mary. Then they both laughed. Cassie had not yet heard Margaret Mary laugh. It was very loud and noisy, and it seemed to bounce off the clean painted walls and tumble around the neat room. The idea of Margaret Mary, proper and prim, laughing like someone's uncle made Cassie laugh even harder. They rolled around on the bed, their arms clasped over their stomachs, gasping, sitting up to look at each other, then collapsing again.

"What are we laughing about?" asked Margaret Mary, trying to look serious. This made them laugh more.

After a while, Cassie sat up, drying her eyes. Margaret Mary sat up next to her, both of them quiet, shy again, looking at their feet. Cassie stared at her sneakers, one taped over a toe, white shoelaces in one, brown in the other. Then she looked at Margaret Mary's feet: pink socks with lace edgings, brown shoes with straps hooked over pearl buttons.

Cassie sighed.

"You have matching clothes," she announced.

Margaret Mary nodded.

"And ribbons and dresses," Cassie added. She got up and walked over to the closet where Margaret Mary's dresses hung in neat rows, one to a hanger. Matching ribbons hung on a hook just inside the closet.

"Maybe I should try matching ribbons," she said thoughtfully.

Margaret Mary reached over Cassie's shoulder, picking out two green ribbons. Together, they stood in front of the mirror, Margaret Mary trying to gather the wild wisps of Cassie's hair into a pigtail on one side, Cassie the other. Her arm up, Cassie could see that there was a hole in the underarm of her shirt. They stood, side by side, looking at their reflections. Margaret Mary tipped her head, studying Cassie. Cassie tried to smile at herself, but she couldn't.

"I look," she said sadly, "like a package."

"Cassie," said Margaret Mary, "your hair is splendid and free. It shouldn't be tied up in ribbons." Then, seeing Cassie's sad look, she added, "They're only ribbons, Cass." She bent her head toward the closet. "They're only dresses. They're *only* socks."

21

Slowly, Cassie reached up and untied the green ribbons. She handed them to Margaret Mary.

"But everything here is so neat and uncluttered," she said, watching Margaret Mary hang the ribbons back on the hook.

"And safe," she added softly, surprising herself.

Margaret Mary put her hand on Cassie's shoulder and they looked at each other in the mirror, Margaret Mary so slim and fair-haired, Cassie, her hair so wild, her eyes sad.

"Only safe and uncluttered on the outside, Cass," said Margaret Mary softly. She gestured. "This is all the outside. It doesn't matter. It only matters if you're safe and uncluttered on the inside."

Inside, outside, thought Cassie as she went to Margaret Mary's bathroom. Closing the door behind her, she saw that Margaret Mary was right about the bathroom. It was nice. There were no hairs in the sink, no remnants of soap bars to be scratched off. The lid of the clothes hamper was closed tightly, not like in Cassie's house where the clothes tumbled out and around and behind. Cassie sat on the edge of the bathtub and leaned over to open the hamper with one finger. At the bottom, very neatly folded, was one blouse. Cassie picked it up. It was not dirty.

Inside, outside, Cassie repeated silently as she and Margaret Mary walked beside the evening sea toward Cassie's house. She didn't understand. It didn't have anything to do with her insides. If Cassie's family would only move back where they lived before, things would be all right again, wouldn't they? Things would be uncluttered. Things would be safe, the way they had been. Cassie thought about Papa. Or would they? The gentle waves along the inlet reached for their bare feet. The stars were scattered across the sky. Cassie watched Margaret Mary, walking beside her. Cassie straightened up and practiced walking delicately, one foot carefully in front of the other, like Margaret Mary. *"Inside, outside, inside, outside, inside, outside,"* she whispered to the rhythm of her steps as she walked home, trying to understand the meaning of Margaret Mary's message.

4

Gran

CASSIE AWOKE LATE the next morning. The sun was high, and Cassie sat on the edge of her bed, thinking about Margaret Mary. She reached for her thesaurus and took out her notebook and pen. *Margaret Mary,* she wrote: *proper, perfect.* She frowned a bit, thinking of Margaret Mary's wild laughter. *Confusing, mysterious,* she added.

"Cass," her mother's voice came up the stairs. "You're late getting up today. Are you all right?"

"Fine," called Cassie.

"I'll need help." She could hear her mother coming up the stairs. "Gran's coming tonight."

24

Her mother stood there, filling the doorway.

Gran. Cassie's heart began to pound. She had forgotten. No, not really forgotten. Gran had always been there on the edges of each day, like the memory. And like the dream that had begun to blur the memory.

"Maybe you could wear the shirt she sent you, the one with the embroidery? She'd like that."

Cassie nodded. Her mother paused, looking at her, her eyes bright and sharp, like Gran's. But she said nothing, and after a moment, she left.

Cassie walked slowly to the closet and took down a blue denim shirt. She held it up and looked at the many stitched memories on it that Gran had sewn for her. A large tree, her tree back home. A rose, one that she and Papa had grown and tended together. "Dang rose!" Papa had yelled at it once. At her surprised look he had explained, "Flowers need stern words. Everything needs stern words at one time or another." A small rowboat, light blue, that she and Gran had rowed together on the back pond, talking and trailing their fingers in the water, watching the turtles sunning, then slipping into the water when they rowed near. A candy box with a red ribbon. Cassie smiled, thinking of the chocolates that she and Gran had always eaten, hidden, in secret places. Once in the backseat of her mother's car, Gran and Cassie had stuffed them greedily into their mouths, warm and melting from the box. "What are you eating?" her mother had asked. "Remember, no snacks before dinner." "Why, we know that, Kate," her Gran had said matter-of-factly. "Celery sticks and carrots," she had replied, making Cassie giggle. "But I hear no crunching!" Cassie's mother had insisted, trying to look at them in the rearview mirror while Cassie and Gran burst into laughter, happily locked into a secret of their own.

Cassie sighed and tried on the shirt. She looked at herself in the mirror for a moment, then she took out her notebook with her poem "Spaces" in it. She read the first two verses, then she wrote:

> *My clothes are spaces, too: a shirt,*
> *My pants*
> *My socks*
> *A dress*
> *A skirt,*
> *And in my shoes, below my clothes*
> *Are spaces there*
> > *for*
> > *all*
> > *my*
> > *toes.*

Not good verse, she thought. But not bad either. Fair to middling, she thought, remembering one of Gran's expressions. As she slipped the notebook back in her drawer, she saw the two tissue-wrapped packages that she had almost forgotten were there. Her hand stopped over one. It was the grandfather doll that had once belonged to her dollhouse. When Papa had died, she had taken it out of the dollhouse and wrapped it up, hiding it in the back of her drawer. She reached in and picked up the other package and slowly unwrapped the wrinkled paper and took out a new doll in a velvet dress with a long white apron trimmed in ribbon. A grandmother doll with gray hair pulled back in a black band. Cassie thought about her Gran who, unlike the doll, insisted on wearing jeans most of the time, and boots or sneakers.

Cassie walked over and stared at her dollhouse. Though the dollhouse was old, the doll family was new and perfect. A mother, a father, two brothers, and a girl. They were dressed in soft and proper clothes and were all in their places. Cassie had always loved moving them around, putting them where they belonged; the mother in a long lavender dress in the dining room with her china dishes, the father before the fireplace reading a book, the brothers in their rooms. And the girl? Cassie moved the girl about, from one room to another, but there was never a right place. Cassie sighed and picked up the girl doll. The grandmother doll in one hand, the girl in the other, she held them in front of her, as if weighing them. Finally, after peering into each room, she shook her head. She put the girl doll in her pocket. Then, lifting her shoulders in a small shrug, she leaned the grandmother doll against the front door, where the doll, patient and silent, waited for someone to let her in.

"Mom, how will Gran be?" Cassie and her mother, both hot from the sun, dressed in old clothes, had been cleaning the cottage that sat high on the bluff.

Cassie's mother straightened up, the cleaning cloth in her hand.

"Be?" she asked. "Be," she repeated again, and Cassie could see that her mother understood, for her face softened.

"Gran will be just as Gran has always been, Cass," she said. "It is Gran's life that has changed some, not Gran."

Cassie, not understanding, shook her head. Her mother took her hand and led her outside, the two of them sitting on the stone steps.

"It has been hardest for you in one way, Cass, because you have not seen Gran since Papa died. Or spoken to her. But I have. Gran is the same. Something has gone from her life, it's true, but she is still Gran. Her life has shifted a bit. Moved." Cassie's mother turned Cassie's hand over, looking at the palm as if reading something there. "A new pattern, Cass."

Cassie stared at her mother, unable to answer, afraid she would cry, half wishing she could.

"Poor Cass," murmured her mother, pulling her close. "Poor Cass, who wishes that things never changed."

Maybe, thought Cassie, her face buried in her mother's shoulder, things wouldn't have changed. Maybe if I'd told Papa I was sorry for yelling, he would still be here. Maybe. Maybe. But these were words she couldn't say. Not ever.

Gently, Cassie pulled away from her mother. "When is Gran coming?"

"After fishing," said her mother, "Dad will bring her." She looked at the sun. "I'd better get to work, Cass. You can stop if you want. Go see Margaret Mary. You've worked hard enough."

Cassie shook her head and watched her mother. There was a smudge across her forehead and her long wild hair had tangled in a gold earring. She looked like a happy gypsy, and Cassie smiled.

"I'll stay and help," she said. She turned and looked out at the ocean, beyond the inlet, trying to see this place as her mother did. But as hard as she tried, she couldn't.

It was later, much later, when all the hardest work was done and Cassie was setting the table for dinner, that she heard the sound of the truck coming up the hill. She ran to the window, watching. Her brothers unloaded the fishing gear and lobster pots from the back. Her father opened the truck door and helped Gran down from the high seat. Gran, with her gray hair tied back with a ribbon, and her long legs, like Cassie's and her mother's, in jeans.

And then, the kitchen door swung open, bringing in the sea wind and her family and Gran. John Thomas caught Cassie up in his arms and whirled her up to the ceiling, where in spite of the clamor of the kitchen, Cassie suddenly felt exposed and alone. She saw Gran's sharp eyes looking at her. For a moment, she surprised John Thomas with unexpected affection, burying her face in his neck, hiding in the smell of the sea. Then he put her down and she went to hug Gran.

"Oh Gran," whispered Cassie, the words suddenly flowing from her like high-tide water going up and over a dune. "I'm sorry . . ."

"Sorry?" said Gran in a crisp voice. "Surely not sorry that I'm here?" She pushed Cassie back to look at her. "Sorry that you seem to be more beautiful? Sorry for this slanted floor? What *is* the matter with this floor, Kate? Sorry that we have lots of time to go rowing and talk?" She bent down and whispered in Cassie's ear, "I have chocolates." Then louder, "No. There's plenty of time to be sorry. Right now I must change clothes and unpack and have a snack of celery sticks and carrots. Upstairs. Coming?" She paused and looked at Cassie.

Cassie laughed suddenly, a sound that startled her. It was all right. Gran was still Gran. And, Cassie thought, as she followed Gran up the stairs, right after supper I must put the grandmother doll where I know it belongs. Inside the dollhouse.

5

Wishes

GRAN AND CASSIE sat in the lee of a dune, the sun warm on their legs, watching the faraway figure of Margaret Mary approach. Cassie knew it was Margaret Mary because of the wind. It was blowing hard, and sometimes Margaret Mary's braids stood out straight behind her.

"I like the wind," said Gran. "It's like someone's trying to talk to me."

Cassie thought about the rattling of the windows in the old house at night and how she hated it, covering her ears, trying to hide beneath the bedcovers.

"You're really different," said Cassie, looking at Gran.

"Different-changed or different-unusual?" asked Gran, a handful of sand sifting through her fingers.

"Different-unusual," said Cassie.

"Well, I should hope so," replied Gran matter-of-factly.

Cassie watched Margaret Mary's slow progress around the bend of the inlet.

"Margaret Mary's different-unusual, too," she said. "She wears socks that match her dresses and speaks with an English accent." Cassie looked sideways at Gran. "And her mother wears high-heeled shoes that make clicking sounds, and she has plastic flowers. They are beautiful. All the time."

Cassie waited and Gran looked at her quizzically.

"Is this some kind of test?" she asked.

Cassie frowned. "I just wondered what you'd think."

"Not really," observed Gran. "You're telling me what *you* think."

Cassie was irked, and there was a long silence while they watched Margaret Mary bend down and pick up something from a tidal pool. A black-backed gull wheeled directly overhead, its lonely croak startling them both. The clouds parted and the sun shone suddenly. Cassie shaded her eyes with her hand and looked at Gran, stretched out beside her. The sun sat cruelly on Gran's face, outlining the wrinkles and the folds of skin under her chin. *Why,* thought Cassie with fear crawling up her spine, *she's an old woman.* She remembered thinking that her Gran was the most beautiful thing in the world, her hair in soft folds swept up on her head, her skin soft and smooth. Now all of that was gone. Cassie remembered her mother's words, "Poor Cass, who wishes that things never changed." Cassie did wish that. She wished it now and always.

"Yes, I have wrinkles," said Gran. She had opened her eyes and was looking at Cassie. "And I am getting old faster than you are."

Cassie flushed and moved uncomfortably. Gran put her hand over Cassie's and Cassie could see that the once smooth hand was now gnarled, the veins making ugly blue roads.

A shadow fell over them, and they looked up to see Margaret Mary standing above them, her head outlined in the sun. Cassie scrambled up, grateful for the interruption.

"This is Margaret Mary."

"And you're Cassie's grand-mum," said Margaret Mary, smiling.

"Sit down, Margaret Mary," said Gran. "We were just talking about wishes."

Cassie looked sharply at Gran. *Were they? How did she know? How could she see?*

Margaret Mary dove, headlong, dress and socks

34

and all, into the dune and rolled over.

"Wishes?" she said. "I have lots. I wish for hamburgers daily, fresh rhubarb, and to do something brave and wonderful."

"Do you have wishes, Gran?" asked Cassie.

"I used to, Cass. I seem to have used them all up by now, except for one or two. I can remember wishing to be a Royal Canadian Mountie when I was your age."

"You did?" exclaimed Margaret Mary, enviously. "I wish I had thought of that wish."

"You may have it," said Gran kindly. She turned on her side. "What do you have there, Margaret Mary?"

Margaret Mary opened her hand. "A creature of some sort," she said. "I found it down there." She pointed toward the inlet.

"A hermit crab," said Gran, smiling.

Margaret Mary put it down on the sand and the bunch of legs emerged from the shell, pushing it along. The crab traveled fast, as if it had somewhere to go, a mission all its own, safe and secure in its shell.

Cassie thought about her poem "Spaces." She had read the first three verses to Gran the first night she had come. Gran had listened, tilting her head slightly to one side, just like Cassie's mother. But when Cassie had finished Gran had only smiled at her.

35

"That's all I've got," Cassie had explained.

"You'll have more," Gran had said.

Cassie stared at the hermit crab. She looked at Gran.

"I've got another verse to 'Spaces,'" she said.

Gran looked at her. "Well then, read it to us."

Cassie reached into her pocket and took out a crumpled piece of paper. She read:

"Outside, my spaces are things that grow:
    A tree,
    A bush,
    A hill of snow.
    (Except for rocks that, as I grow taller,
     Seem to shrink and grow much smaller)
I listen, hear, and stop to see.
And no one ever knows it's me.

    "'Hear that?' they say. 'A hare, a bird!'
     When it's really me, the noise they've heard."

She looked at Margaret Mary, then Gran.

"What do you think?"

"I like it," said Margaret Mary briskly.

Cassie looked at Gran.

"It's not finished," said Gran.

Cassie frowned as Gran picked up the hermit crab.

"But what do you think?"

"See this?" Gran held up the hermit crab. "Do

36

you know that the hermit crab changes shells as he grows? He doesn't live in the same space all his life."

"You never answer questions," said Cassie grumpily. "I asked you what you thought of the poem."

"Maybe she did answer you," said Margaret Mary after a moment.

Gran smiled and put her arm over her eyes.

Cassie, angry with the both of them, turned over onto her belly and watched the hermit crab. Wishes? Cassie had many wishes. She wished to be away from here, back home where everything stayed the same. She wished for everything to be perfect. But right now, under the bright sun, Cassie wished most to be the hermit crab, happily carrying his space around with him.

6

Kaleidoscope

IT WAS ON THE WEDNESDAY after Gran's arrival that Margaret Mary ceased to be a comfortable mystery to Cassie. It was Margaret Mary's first dinner at Cassie's house, and if Margaret Mary's raucous laughter had not fit with the character that Cassie had wished her to be, it became clear that Margaret Mary herself was not as she had first appeared to be. For neat and combed, saying "Mum" for Mom, using phrases like "very regrettably," and wearing her lace-edged socks, Margaret Mary also knew all the questionable words in the dictionary.

"Hair ball!" she shrieked, collapsing on Cassie's bed, her finger still marking the place in Webster's.

Cassie, standing in front of her mirror and trying in vain once more to make her curly hair lie down like Margaret Mary's, was astounded. And upset. She had gone through a lot of trouble with her family, preparing for Margaret Mary's first visit.

"Put on your shoes," she had hissed to her mother.

"Could you wear a dress, Gran?

"Please wear your tweed jacket?" she pleaded to her father.

"Who are we trying to be?" demanded John Thomas.

"Brainless," whispered James.

"I may wear a dress," her Gran muttered stubbornly. "I may not."

Cassie had walked to Margaret Mary's house to get her, and Margaret Mary's mother had opened the door, looking wonderfully serene. She wore a clump of luminescent pearl earrings that looked as if they might glow in the dark. She had a spray bottle and had been cleaning her plastic plants. The room smelled faintly of cleanser.

Margaret Mary, dressed in a pink dress, surprised Cassie right away. She had cursed twice on the way to Cassie's house. One damn and two hells in a row. Cassie had spent a good part of their walk mulling this over, trying to fit the new

Margaret Mary into her picture of the old. She had not managed it by the time they got to Cassie's front door.

"Oh good, your mum's got no shoes," said Margaret Mary when she was introduced. And as Cassie frowned at her mother, Margaret Mary sat down on the rag rug and removed her shoes.

And now, in the upstairs room, padding about in her socks, Margaret Mary didn't even look like Margaret Mary anymore. She was a stranger.

"Oh yes, I am very fond of the word *hair ball*," repeated Margaret Mary. "Remind me, won't you? I've no pencil. Two words it is. Comes between hair and hairbreadth." Margaret Mary leaned over the dictionary, intently studying her new word.

"Your socks," said Cassie weakly, having no idea what to say to this new Margaret Mary, "they are wonderful." And with a sigh, Cassie took Margaret Mary down to dinner, only the smallest hope remaining that Margaret Mary would civilize Cassie's family.

But Margaret Mary proved a traitor. She loved fish, for one thing.

"We never have it," she explained to Cassie's father. "It makes my mother break out in the bumps and honk a lot."

"No fish?" asked James, amazed. "What do you eat then?"

"Lots of casseroles cooked in slop sauce, very

regrettably," announced Margaret Mary, thereby removing Cassie's last hope for an elegant dinner.

Margaret Mary also loved Cassie's house.

"It's lovely," she commented in her clipped way of speaking, "the way your floors tip a bit. And your plants! Are they real?"

Cassie's mother smiled at her. "Yes, they are real. All of them."

"I like that one best of all," Margaret Mary said, pointing. "The one that looks like a pine tree."

"That's rosemary," said Gran who had been watching Cassie watch Margaret Mary. "Rosemary for remembrance. It's an herb."

Margaret Mary nodded. "We have lots of herbs in England. I think most of them began as weeds." She beamed at John Thomas and James, who beamed back. "Maybe that's why my mum likes plastic plants," she added thoughtfully. "She hates weeds."

Margaret Mary even loved the Jell-O dessert that wasn't quite Jell-O yet.

"I say," said Margaret Mary admiringly, "one could almost suck this through a straw, couldn't one?"

Cassie sighed heavily. One could all right, she thought, devastated. And she stared at Margaret Mary, happily slurping her runny Jell-O dessert and wiggling her stockinged toes beneath the table.

Most of all, Margaret Mary loved Cassie's family and the talk of boats and fishing. And the sea.

"What's it like," she asked James, "to be out there? Are you the only boat you can see?"

James, his face touched by the glow of the lamp, his eyes narrowed as if focused on a faraway view, told Margaret Mary.

"Sometimes alone, most times one of many. It's like a giant, or something bigger than all of us, has taken the sky and tucked it down securely all around and kept us safely bobbing within."

Cassie, her fork caught midway between her plate and her mouth, stared at James. She'd never heard him talk this way before. Or seen his look of contentment.

"But there are storms!" she protested as everyone turned to look at her.

Her father laughed. "That there are, Cass," he said.

"But after the storms," said John Thomas, smiling, "coming home with the gulls and terns following us, some even daring to sit on the boat, waiting for scraps of fish, it is like . . ." John Thomas, not used to long speeches, searched for the right words.

"Peace," said James quietly. "It is peace."

"And," said Cassie's father, as if adding to a chorus, "that's the way it has been for hundreds and hundreds of years. Just the men, the boats, and the sea."

There was a long silence. It had never occurred to Cassie that they loved fishing. She had always thought they did it because they had to.

"It is somehow always the same and yet never the same," said Cassie's father. "But always beautiful."

"Like a kaleidoscope!" exclaimed Margaret Mary. She turned to Cassie. "Do you have one?" Then, not stopping for Cassie's answer, she went on. "When I was very little, in England, I had one. I would turn it and turn it and the pieces of glass would fall into patterns, all lovely. But I would want one pattern—one special one—to stay there forever. But the pieces of glass would fall into another shape, then another. And they were never the same."

"But always beautiful," said Cassie's mother softly.

"I remember," said Cassie. "I always wanted one to stay the same for always."

"And you still do," said Gran.

Cassie stared at Gran. Then she broke the silence. "Fish stink sometimes, you know."

She had not meant the harsh flatness of the statement, but everyone knew it, for they laughed.

"Everything stinks sometimes," announced

43

Margaret Mary. "You ought to smell my mother's casseroles."

They laughed harder, and got up to clear away the dishes, all but Cassie in bare feet or socks.

Afterward, sitting on the porch, listening to the steady lap and swish of the waves, they sang while Cassie's mother played the flute. Rounds at first, and one that Margaret Mary made them sing over and over again. *"Dona Nobis Pacem."*

"It's splendid," said Margaret Mary. "What does it mean?"

Cassie's mother smiled. "It means Grant us peace," she said.

Peace. The word tumbled through Cassie's thoughts. Peace, her brothers had said. She thought about her grandfather. Peace.

"Let's sing something happy," said Cassie, her voice sounding lost in her throat.

"No, please, once more," said Margaret Mary. "It *is* happy. What's happier than peace?"

They sang it again, this time Margaret Mary singing, too, her voice clear and light.

"Margaret Mary, you have a wonderful voice," said Cassie's mother.

"Yes," said Margaret Mary, looking surprised, making them all smile, "I do, don't I?"

A cloud drifted over the moon, and Cassie's father yawned.

"I'll walk you home," said Cassie.

"Wait. Before you go I have a gift for you." Cassie's mother disappeared into the kitchen and came back with the pot of rosemary. "Here. A real plant for a real girl."

Margaret Mary smiled and buried her face in the plant.

"It smells like the sea," she said, her voice muffled.

A real plant with dirt in the pot, thought Cassie, embarrassed. Why would Margaret Mary want that when she had a jungle of plastic plants, all perfect, every day the same, at home? But Margaret Mary was delighted.

It was low tide, and Margaret Mary and Cassie walked home, barefoot, on the cool wet sand.

"Your family is splendid," said Margaret Mary. "Splendid."

Cassie smiled at the word. It was not the word she would choose for her family. There were other words she had written on her paper list: *wild, raucous, infuriating, maddening, eccentric . . .*

"Thanks, Cass," said Margaret Mary at her front door. "Shall we meet at the big dune tomorrow?"

Cassie nodded and watched her walk into the house, turning off the light behind her. Cassie stood for a moment. Then, as she turned to leave, an upstairs window opened and Margaret Mary leaned out.

"You are splendid, too, Cass!" she called to Cassie. "Here." She threw something down, something small and light colored, that fell at Cassie's feet. As the upstairs window closed again, Cassie bent down and saw what it was. It was Margaret Mary's pink lace-edged socks, rolled neatly into a ball.

Cassie smiled all the way home, although she didn't know why. The pieces didn't fit together for her. They kept shifting, first one way, then another. But one thing was certain—she had a friend. That night, before falling asleep, her head was filled with changing patterns, each different, each beautiful. Like the kaleidoscope. And before morning light touched her awake, she had gotten one of her wishes. She had slept a sleep without dreams.

7

Feathers and Rhymes

CASSIE'S RELATIVES BURST forth like clowns out of a circus car, tumbling and tripping over each other. Cousin Coralinda, wearing her feathered cape, carried her baby; Uncle Hat carried his suitcase, his telescope, and his bag of surplus hats. The wind was fierce, and Cassie had visions of Cousin Coralinda taking flight, her feathered cape lifting her high above their heads. The binoculars around Hat's neck kept him firmly anchored, and he opened the door to the back seat, letting out Bumble Bee and Bitsy. Bumble Bee was a large and exuberant sheep dog, and unless he was eating or going to the bathroom, it was hard to tell which end was which. Cassie put out her hand to pet him, and Bumble Bee, as always, immediately fell on his back with his legs in the air, asking for stomach rubs. Bitsy, Cousin Coralinda's cat, had a risky nature. She purred and rubbed and snarled and bit those she loved. Poor Hat bore the scars of many affectionate attacks.

Cousin Coralinda set down her baby, Baby Binnie as she was called. "As if," Gran had once said, "anyone might forget she was a baby. Labeled, you might say."

"Hello, hello," burbled Cousin Coralinda, kissing her finger, then touching Cassie's cheek, as if avoiding germs.

"Blamsch," said Baby Binnie.

"That's 'hello,' " said Cousin Coralinda.

Cassie smiled at Baby Binnie and Baby Binnie smiled back, a rather long festoon of spit falling out her mouth and down her chin.

Margaret Mary, invited for the arrival, was in awe. Cassie noted, with amusement, that her jaw hung open a bit.

"Oooh, Margaret Mary. How lovely. . . ." Cousin Coralinda's voice trailed off, and so did Cousin Coralinda. Cousin Coralinda had a high forehead and a strong jaw and lots of white teeth. She looked, Cassie thought, like a rather nice horse. Cousin Coralinda didn't move like a horse, however. She moved, as James once described it, as if she were on wheels. "She'll appear at your elbow, out of nowhere, and ask a question," he said. "You'll stop to answer, and then, when you look up again, she's silently rolled away."

Cassie smiled. Even in sand, she noticed, Cousin Coralinda could roll.

"Twelve and two/Good to see you," said Uncle Hat, smiling at Cassie. Cassie couldn't think of a rhyme quickly, but Margaret Mary, prepared for Hat, did.

"One and three/You're good to see," she said, and Hat smiled and shook her hand solemnly. He handed Cassie and Margaret Mary the smaller pieces of luggage, and they began carrying them to the cottage on the bluff.

"Why does he wear hats?" whispered Margaret Mary.

"Don't know," said Cassie, putting Hat's telescope over her shoulder. "It's a mystery. He even wears a hat to bed."

"Did anyone ever ask him?" asked Margaret Mary.

Cassie stopped suddenly to stare at Margaret Mary. No one ever had that Cassie knew of. But it was like Margaret Mary to think of it. "The fastest way between two points," Margaret Mary once said, "is a straight line." And a direct question was a straight line.

"I'm sure it is something drastic and complicated, dark and drear," said Cassie. "Too horrible to be mentioned."

"Dark and drear?" asked Margaret Mary.

"Maybe he's embarrassed about his head," said Cassie, thoughtfully.

"Or," said Margaret Mary, "he was denied hats as a child by his mother, now departed."

They both laughed. Then Cassie sighed.

"I wish they were normal," she said fervently.

"More wishes?" Margaret Mary lifted her eyebrows.

"Well, you know"—Cassie waved a hand—"you've seen them. They're . . . they're . . . different."

It was Margaret Mary's turn to sigh. "I know," she said enviously. "It's wonderful. Splendid." That word again. "I wish . . ." Her voice stopped. "I do wish that I had some abnormal family."

"You do?"

Margaret Mary nodded. "All I've got is an aunt in Sussex who sweeps the floor constantly and wears a tea cozy on her head."

Cassie and Margaret Mary looked at each other and burst out laughing.

"Wishes," said Margaret Mary, giggling.

"Wishes," echoed Cassie, smiling broadly.

And they went off to deliver all the luggage while Bumble Bee loped and sniffed and rolled about the sea roses, and Bitsy jumped at their shoelaces and furiously attacked Cousin Coralinda's feathered cape.

Cousin Coralinda, unaware, had provided Cassie with a wonderful new hiding place. She had brought a huge and horrible tablecloth as a gift for Cassie's mother—white with windy swirls of green and birds in every color. It was close to the ugliest thing Cassie had seen or imagined, but Cassie's mother loved it.

"It's different and unique," she insisted admiringly, throwing the bright cloth out and letting it settle like a parachute over the oak table in the dining room.

It was different all right, thought Cassie. Just like everything and everyone here. Feathers and rhymes and too much of both. But as soon as Cassie had seen that the tablecloth touched the floor all around, she knew at once that it was for her. A space of her own. She could hardly wait for dinner to be over and done with so she could creep in and hide under the tablecloth to listen and watch.

Dinner was striped bass on a large platter with parsley and lemon slices.

"I would wish/for lots more fish," rhymed Hat.

51

"Oogmits," said Baby Binnie from her high chair, her face serious and serene.

"That's 'milk'!" exclaimed Cousin Coralinda happily. "Didn't you hear?" The feather boa that she wore around her neck rippled with the drafts from the open window. One feather flew loose as James and John Thomas smiled into their glasses of milk.

Bumble Bee snored, stretched out on the kitchen floor, and Bitsy lurked ominously beneath the table, alternately rubbing against their legs and pouncing painfully on their feet.

"Oh," exclaimed Cousin Coralinda, "dessert is ice cream! Say ice cream, Baby Binnie."

"Ribbish," said Baby Binnie, happily allowing mashed potatoes to ooze out of the corners of her mouth.

"That's wonderful!" cried Cousin Coralinda.

"Glanx?" asked Baby Binnie, lovingly winding her fingers with Gran's.

It was not until the next day that Cassie found a time to be under the tablecloth, for dinner was too long and Cassie too weary to explore. As it turned out, Cassie would always remember her first time in her new space, the early morning light making it a cave of color. For it was on August 12, at 8:22, that Cassie Binegar (whose name rhymes with vinegar) fell in love.

8

Feet

ACTUALLY, IT WAS NOT the writer himself but his feet that Cassie loved first. During the next month, she was to become quite familiar with many pairs of feet from her space under the tablecloth. She recognized all the voices, but it was the feet she came to know, almost as if each person was turned upside down for her. And what the voice said was not always what the feet said to Cassie. Uncle Hat's, planted firmly with a once-in-a-while covering of one with the other; Gran's, long and blue veined and restless; her mother's, brown and

53

relaxed; Coralinda's, prim and parked neatly; her brothers', up and down and never there for long; her father's, happily stretching, small tufts of black hair on each toe. Baby Binnie's didn't reach, of course, the only evidence of her the soggy bits of food dropped from her high chair. Feet told Cassie more than mouths or minds or words, and from time to time, Cassie would take off her socks and shoes and try to read her own feet.

It was the morning of August 12, early, that Cassie came to know the writer's feet. Sitting silently beneath the tablecloth, listening to the comings and goings and murmurings of her mother and Gran, daydreaming happily, she was not even aware of the knock at the door. Suddenly the writer's feet were there, booted, one foot thrust back under his chair as he sat, the other thrown out, just missing Cassie.

"I'd appreciate it if you could rent me a cottage," his soft voice said, and in accompaniment, his feet moved. "I write for the newspaper, but I'm taking off a month or two to write for myself. I need a space."

A space. Her word, thought Cassie as she sat up straighter.

He sighed and his feet curled a bit, sighing with him. "I'm tired of writing about births, deaths, trips to nowhere, and hardware sales," he said.

54

"You may find," said Gran crisply, "that those are the things you will write about anyway."

Cassie frowned, but the writer laughed.

"I wonder," said Cassie's mother thoughtfully. "We could rent you the smallest cottage. Only for a month or two, though, or through October. There isn't heat, you know."

"That would be splendid," he said happily, his feet agreeing.

Splendid. Margaret Mary's word.

"I cook for myself," he went on, "and I could do some work for you in my spare time."

Beneath the tablecloth, Cassie longed to see his face. A writer, think of it! Right here. Her face felt warm. She remembered feeling this way only once, in the fourth grade, and then it had only lasted for a day and a half. She had loved Mr. Bagg, her teacher, on sight. Loved him until his sharp-faced wife came to school, dragging along two horrible children, one who stuck his tongue out behind poor Mr. Bagg's back, the other with a suspicious smell about his pants.

All of a sudden the feet disappeared; Gran's, her mother's, and the writer's.

"I'll bring my things in a day or two," he said, standing close to the table. Cassie could see the outline of his leg leaning into the cloth.

"I'll have the cottage ready," Cassie's mother

said. "You'll have to bring sheets and towels."

That's wonderful, thought Cassie. A writer actually bringing his sheets and towels to our cottage.

"Say," Cousin Coralinda's voice called in the front door. "I've lost Bitsy. Is she in here?"

"Bitsy?" asked the writer.

"A cat," said Gran. There was a flurry of activity as they called and searched for Bitsy.

"I'll keep looking outside," called Cousin Coralinda, and the door banged shut.

"Does she come when she's called?" asked the writer. "Perhaps under the tablecloth," he added.

Underneath, Cassie sat very still. She could feel the pounding of her heart. And then the tablecloth was pulled up and Cassie was staring into the writer's face. *He has no beard,* thought Cassie wildly. *I thought all writers have beards.* For a moment there was a silence as Cassie stared at the writer and he stared back, his dark eyes steady, a slight smile on his face. And then the tablecloth dropped again.

"No cat," said the writer, matter-of-factly. And then more softly he repeated, "No cat."

Sudden tears came to Cassie's eyes. Shame at being discovered, at being caught. But then, as they all walked out the door to look for Bitsy and Cassie was left alone, another thought overwhelmed her. She had loved his feet first. But now, thought Cassie happily, I love his face as

56

well. And she sat, her arms around her knees, for a long time in her new space.

Fast as the wind, Cassie ran down the dunes and over the hard-packed edges of the inlet to Margaret Mary's house. Margaret Mary and her mother were outside, weeding around the neat privet hedge. Margaret Mary's mother had a headful of shocking-pink rollers, and she looked like a huge bloom. Cassie stared at her for a moment before she remembered the news.

"Margaret Mary, there's a writer going to live in the small cottage!"

Breathless, Cassie fell to the grass.

"What sort of rider?" asked Margaret Mary, shading her eyes. "Horse? Or motorcycle?"

"Writer!" exclaimed Cassie. "Not rider. He's written for the newspaper but he's tired of writing about births, deaths, trips to nowhere, and hardware sales. Now he's going to write something for himself."

"A pity, actually," said Margaret Mary's mother, looking up. "I am most fond of reading about hardware sales."

"Does he have a beard?" asked Margaret Mary, warming to the subject.

"No beard," said Cassie. "But he'll be bringing his sheets and towels to the cottage. In a day or two."

"That's jolly," proclaimed Margaret Mary. "His own sheets and towels."

Cassie began to laugh.

"It is that," she said, imitating Margaret Mary. "It is jolly."

"Well, dirt and weeds are not jolly," complained Margaret Mary's mother, holding up some wild honeysuckle by her thumb and first finger as if she held a rotten fish. "This weed is not jolly."

This made Margaret Mary and Cassie tumble around and peal with laughter. They ran down to the inlet and pranced in the water, sending up the shore birds and getting the bottoms of their pants wet.

"Jolly!" shouted Cassie to the wind, thinking she'd never felt so happy.

And like an echo, Margaret Mary's voice repeated, "Jolly, jolly, jolly."

9

Conversations

IN THE COOL AND DARK and private place beneath the tablecloth Cassie became ears, hearing information and thoughts that she would not have if she hadn't hidden there. Only once did the idea of hiding make her uncomfortable, and that was when she told Margaret Mary about being there when the writer had come.

"Hidden!" Margaret Mary was shocked. "That's not good, Cassie. Not good. There are some things not meant to be heard by hidden ears. How would *you* feel if someone spied on you?"

Cassie had dropped the subject. It was, of course,

59

absurd to think that anyone else would ever hide under the table. Or that any grown-up would hide at all, and listen. And it wasn't really spying, thought Cassie. It was only listening. And learning. In order to be a better writer. Yes, that was it, Cassie reasoned. It made good sense. But she had never talked about it again with Margaret Mary. She cared what Margaret Mary thought of her. And what Gran thought. Strangely alike, the two of them. And now the writer, thought Cassie with some fear. He was to come in two days. What would *he* think of her, hiding beneath the table-cloth? He knew. He had seen. But neither Margaret Mary's warnings or her own fears stopped Cassie. She sat and hid. And listened.

"Poor Cousin Cor," her Gran's voice came to her from above. "Her husband flew the coop."

Flew the coop? Cassie knew that meant he left. But the way Gran said it brought to mind a picture of Cor's husband, whoever he was, spreading his wings and flying off, winging over hills and dunes and rivers to a faraway place. Migrating, perhaps.

"Coralinda worries too much," said Cassie's mother, shifting a bit in her chair, her toes fanning out beneath the table.

"Or tries too hard," answered Gran. "Binnie will talk when she wants. She needs to get her mind off Baby Binnie, and off herself."

There was a pause, then the sound of the two of them laughing.

"What were they? Coralinda's first words?" asked Cassie's mother.

"I believe, at age two," said Gran, "her words were 'The picture is slightly tilted on the wall!' "

"No," said Cassie's mother, her voice filled with laughter. "I believe she looked out the window, turned to Uncle Hat, and said 'The road crew has just passed the house.' "

Her voice ended on a high whoop of a note, and she and Gran leaned toward each other, laughing helplessly. They got up, their feet disappearing from under the table, and Cassie lifted the tablecloth and watched them, their arms around each other like small children.

I wish they would stay like this forever, thought Cassie as she dropped the tablecloth and sat and waited, feeling for the first time a bit of a captive beneath the table.

"Who's the man?" asked Cousin Coralinda. "Moving things into the small cottage?" Her feet, in brocade slippers with feathered trim, slipped silently under the table. "Baby Binnie likes him."

Cassie's ears prickled. Of course she liked him. Baby Binnie liked everyone.

"That is Jason," said Cassie's mother, peeling

potatoes over the kitchen sink. "He's going to write."

Jason. Cassie tried the name, silently, only her lips moving. It was a nice name. But to Cassie he was the writer. Would always be THE WRITER.

"Write what?" asked Coralinda. "Say write, Baby Binnie, write."

"Schramp," said Baby Binnie, dropping a piece of toast to the floor. The toast lay close to Cassie, and she moved back waiting for Cousin Cor to reach down and pick it up. Instead, to Cassie's horror, Baby Binnie's fat feet appeared, then Baby Binnie's diapered bottom, then Baby Binnie herself, holding up the tablecloth, peering under.

"Write a novel, I guess," answered Cassie's mother. "Or short stories. He didn't say much about it. Only that he wanted some time and a place. He *is* nice, isn't he?"

Cassie, slowly inching backward, watched as Baby Binnie lifted the tablecloth up, then down, then up, then down, in a private game of hide-and-seek.

"Cass," Baby Binnie said very clearly.

"What?" asked Cousin Coralinda. "What did you say? Toast? Say toast, Binnie."

"Cass," said Baby Binnie, peering right into Cassie's face as Cassie smiled weakly.

"Good girl," said Coralinda. And suddenly

Baby Binnie disappeared to Coralinda's lap as if whisked up and away on an invisible elevator. Cassie breathed a sigh of relief.

"Cor?" Her mother's voice sounded hesitant.

"Yes?"

"It's not really my business," she began, "but are you happy alone?"

"Alone?" Cousin Cor said too brightly. "I'm not alone. I've got Hat and Baby Binnie."

"You know what I mean," Cassie's mother said softly, sliding into a chair, her feet whispering under the table.

Cousin Cor sighed.

"No, I'm not happy. But who would want me, with a baby who won't speak words. And my feathers. Oh yes," she went on, "I know how I look. And I know that Baby Binnie doesn't make sense."

"Oh, Coralinda," said Cassie's mother. "Binnie will talk in time. Give her time."

She said 'Cass,' cried Cassie silently under the table. *Baby Binnie said 'Cass' as clear as could be.*

"And Cor, you wear feathers for the same reason Hat wears hats, don't you know? And talks in rhymes."

There was a silence, then Coralinda's voice so low that Cassie had to turn her head to hear.

"I know," said Coralinda. "I know."

But I don't know, thought Cassie under the table.

Why? She looked down and saw a feather lying by Cousin Cor's foot, fallen from a shoe. Cassie picked it up and smoothed it.

Then there were only the soft burbling sounds of Baby Binnie. Cassie knew that Cousin Cor was crying. Cassie put the feather next to her cheek for comfort. For hers or Cousin Coralinda's, she wondered. And suddenly, for the first time in her life, Cassie wished that she were somewhere else, far away from her safe space. There were still no answers. And what Margaret Mary had said was true. There were some things not meant for hidden ears.

10

Questions and Answers

THE FIRST THING the writer did when he arrived
was to put up a small bird feeder. He hung it
from the porch hook and filled it with sunflower
seeds. Cassie saw this from her perch up a small
pine tree nearby. She had not meant to be up
the tree when he arrived. It had just happened.
And now there was no coming down until he left.

Cassie's mother walked up the path and into
the hidden yard where the small cottage stood.

"Is everything all right?" she called to him.

"Fine." He turned and smiled at her. "First
things first. I'm feeding the birds."

"Come for dinner tonight," said Cassie's mother. "You can meet everyone. Then we'll leave you on your own."

Cassie's mother went off again, humming to herself. When she had disappeared, the writer walked over to the tree and looked up.

"You can come down now, little bird."

Cassie sighed and climbed down the tree.

"I didn't mean it. This time," she added, red-faced.

The writer smiled at her and held out his hand.

"I'm Jason."

"I know. The writer. I'm Cassie." Cassie took his hand. It was long fingered and cool. Now she loved his fingers, too.

"Ah, of course you know. I'd almost forgotten."

"It was nice of you not to say anything," said Cassie.

"You're welcome," said the writer. "You know, hiding is not always a good thing."

"You sound like Margaret Mary," said Cassie.

"And who's Margaret Mary?"

"My friend," explained Cassie. "She's from England and she has plastic plants that her mother sprays with disinfectant and her favorite word is hair ball."

The writer laughed for a long time. I suppose, Cassie thought, resigned, I will now love his teeth. And she did.

66

"Anyway," said Cassie, "she thinks my hiding is not good. But I'm doing it because I want to be a writer, like you. And hiding is the best way to find out what you want to know."

"Not so," said the writer, sitting on the porch steps. "Being a part of it all is the best way."

"But aren't you hiding?" asked Cassie. She waved her arm. "Here?"

"I don't think so," said the writer. "No," he said more positively, "I don't think so at all."

"Margaret Mary says asking questions is the best way to find out," said Cassie.

"True," said the writer.

"Well, sometimes I can't ask questions. Not the right ones."

The writer thought a moment.

"Well, then, since you are going to be a writer, do the next best thing."

"What's that?"

"Write the questions," said the writer.

Write them.

"But who will write back?"

"I'll bet the most important person will," said the writer.

"Who's that?"

"The person who knows the answers," said the writer. He looked closely at Cassie. Finally, he got up and stretched.

"I'm going," said Cassie, knowing that her time

was up. "But before I go, could I ask you one very important and personal question?"

The writer paused, midstretch. "Starting right off? All right." He finished the stretch. "What?"

Cassie wanted to ask if he was married, with a sharp-chinned wife and horrid children; if he loved the color blue; if he liked sunrises or sunsets.

She took a deep breath.

"Do you write with an outline?" she asked in a hurry.

"An outline, an outline!" mimicked the writer, laughing. "Get off with you while I think about it." He picked up some sand and tossed it after her legs as she ran down the path.

I first loved his feet, thought Cassie happily as she went home to begin asking questions. Then I loved his face, then his fingers, then his teeth. Now, thought Cassie, as she ran up the front steps to set the table for dinner, I love his mind. Cassie stopped midway up the stairs with a terrible thought. Oh dear God, thought Cassie, using one of Margaret Mary's expressions, I do hope I love his writing as well.

Very quietly, without fuss, Cassie taped up a large sheet of paper on the bathroom wall. It was the place most likely, she thought, for the person who had the answers to take the time to think about them. And write them down.

QUESTIONS   ANSWERS

Cassie stood back and looked at the neat lettering, the tip of her pencil in her mouth. Finally, she leaned over and wrote under "Questions":

Why don't I have a space of my own?

Then the sounds of the dinner guests below intruded. Cassie stood for a moment on the stairway, watching hidden from above before she went downstairs to become a character in the scene below.

Everyone had brought something for dinner. Gran had baked all day and the kitchen still smelled of homemade bread and cookies. Cassie was overjoyed to see that her mother had roasted a turkey instead of fish. The writer had brought cheese. Uncle Hat brought a kicker.

"What's a kicker?" asked Margaret Mary.

"Wine," said Coralinda, smiling faintly.

"Seven and four/There's always more," said Hat, tipping up his wineglass.

"What are the sticks and weeds in the salad?" asked Cassie.

69

"Sticks and weeds?" Coralinda, flushed from the kitchen, laughed. "Those are herbs and bean sprouts, Cassie."

"Look like sticks and weeds," commented Cassie.

Cassie looked closely at Cousin Coralinda. What was it that was different? She still wore feathers, but the only ones in sight were feather earrings, slightly worn, that made her look a bit as if she were molting. There *was* something different. Something else.

The writer took Baby Binnie on his lap, where she sat staring at him for a long time.

"Baby Binnie, Skinny Binnie," sang the writer, not embarrassed at all. Baby Binnie grinned, her three and a half teeth making her look like a carved pumpkin.

"Ratch," said Baby Binnie to the writer.

"Ratch is right," said the writer, smiling back at Binnie.

"Whatever is that in the bathroom?" asked James, coming into the kitchen.

"What do you mean? What's there?" asked Cassie's mother.

"It looks to me," said Gran, "like a sheet for questions and answers. Put there, I suppose, by someone who wishes to know more. A good idea, I might say."

Cassie grinned at Gran.

70

"You know I put it there," she said.

"It did look like your handwriting," said James, smiling.

"And I was very tired of writing answers on toilet paper," joked John Thomas.

The writer said nothing, but smiled at Cassie from across the table. He turned to Cassie's father.

"Your boat is beautiful," he said.

Cassie saw that her father was pleased.

"You've seen her? Yes, she is beautiful. You like boats?"

The writer nodded. "Never had much of a chance to use them. I grew up in the west, where there is not much water."

Beautiful? Cassie thought about her father's boat, solid and gray with painted decks, the smell of fish never washed away, the windows of the wheelhouse blurred and sticky with salt spray.

Cassie's father sat back and took a sip of his wine. He looked past everyone there, as if reaching for something far away. "I've loved boats forever," he said softly. "When I was seven, I built a raft out of building boards and old nails. Launched it on the river."

Cassie studied him. She had hardly ever thought of him as a boy of seven. What did he look like then? Was he tall or short, curly haired, fair, sad, happy? Was he the same person as now?

After dinner they had cookies and raisin cake

on the porch, the fading sunlight turning the sky the old gold color of late afternoon. It touched the faces of everyone, making them seem unreal, like old photographs: Gran, leaning back in a wicker chair, sipping tea from a china cup; Cassie's brothers arguing gently over the last piece of cake; her mother and father, sitting close together on the couch, the backs of their hands touching; Baby Binnie, sitting at the foot of the steps, eating sand with a spoon. The writer leaned over to say something to Coralinda, and she bent forward eagerly, her hair loose, brushing her cheek. It was then that Cassie saw just what it was that was different about Coralinda. She looked at Margaret Mary and knew, by her look, that Margaret Mary had seen too. Looking more closely, Cassie saw what it was. Cousin Coralinda looked much less like a horse than usual tonight. Cassie wondered if the writer noticed.

After dinner, everyone gone to bed, the writer gone home to his very own sheets and towels, Cassie walked quietly into the upstairs bathroom and turned on the light. There, on the sheet of paper, was something written that had not been there before. The writing was new, tall and straight. Cassie smiled. She knew who had written it. She came closer to read:

Each of us has a space of his own. We carry it around as close as skin, as private as our dreams. What makes you think you don't have your own, too?

Cassie's smiled faded. What did that mean? It was just like the writer to answer a question with another question, thought Cassie.

"He must have been a teacher once," she announced right out loud in the bathroom. No quick answers after all, thought Cassie unhappily. And she turned off the light, leaving herself and the questions in the dark.

11

Cocoons

CASSIE PASSED BY the writer's cottage often, sometimes with real errands, most times with imaginary ones. Some days she could see him at his typewriter by the window, punching away in a two-fingered assault. Other days he was pacing and speaking out loud, gesturing, to no one. But sometimes his listeners were real. Once, Cassie had peered in the window to a scene of littered papers, Baby Binnie in the middle with a pan and a wooden spoon, the writer reading something to Cousin Coralinda. Peering closer, Cassie could see Coralinda, leaning forward as she had at the family dinner, chin in hand, looking rapt—one of Cassie's new words. There were few feathers to be seen, except on Coralinda's shoes. But, looking at the writer, Cassie saw with a prickling sense of dread that he had a feather stuck behind his ear where a pencil might be. Should be. Cassie waited a long time, standing behind a tree, then sitting, until at long last the writer emerged, holding Baby Binnie easily in one arm, his other arm resting gently across Coralinda's shoulders. They had walked along the path, passing whisper near to Cassie.

"It's the character I'm worried about, Cor . . ."

"But there's no need . . ." Cousin Coralinda's voice came, soft.

"Are you sure?" The writer's voice, worried.

"Namnit," announced Baby Binnie, her hands buried in the writer's hair.

Ask me, Cassie cried out silently. *Ask* me. They had disappeared from view then, down the path to Cousin Coralinda's cottage, and Cassie had sat and waited, as if still under the tablecloth. But no one came for her to listen to. Only a chickadee, fearless and friendly, working its way down a branch.

Today, Cassie heard the writer mumbling to himself as he carried a brown paper bag of sunflower seeds for the feeder. Cassie waited behind a tree, watching as he emptied a few seeds into

75

his hand. He stood, hand out, still as a rock, and waited for a chickadee to eat them. Cassie felt a small sound of wings next to her head, and she slowly raised her head to see the bird sit on a branch and watch. And then, there was the sound of the bird leaving the branch. The writer smiled as the chickadee sat for a moment on his hand, then, seed in his beak, he flew off above their heads.

The writer saw Cassie, waiting by the tree, and he smiled and beckoned to her.

"Come, join the chickadees in dinner." He popped a sunflower seed in his mouth. "And me in tea?" He turned and walked up the front porch steps.

"What are you doing out here?" asked Cassie. "You should be writing."

"Writing, dear Cass," said the writer, "is only one part of living, you know. Would you deny me the pleasures of bird life, snacks, nature, the world, and the pleasure of your company?"

"Were you ever a teacher?" asked Cassie abruptly.

The writer laughed. "You can tell, eh?" He disappeared inside the cottage and Cassie stood by the door, looking at the litter. There were books and papers, one paper nearly falling off the table. Cassie stepped gingerly over a pile of books and walked, tiptoe, through a paper path. There was

76

a soft crunching noise under her foot, and she looked down to see a splintered yellow pencil.

The writer came in from the kitchen, then, managing to carry two cups and a kettle of hot water.

"We'll have to share a tea bag," he announced, speaking strangely because the tag end of the tea bag was in his mouth.

Cassie hated tea. Not hated, actually. She found it dull and horrible and in need of something such as four teaspoons of sugar. Somehow, though, the idea of sharing a tea bag with the writer made it sound more interesting. Almost intimate. Or exotic. He put down the cups and the teapot on a pile of papers, and Cassie looked around. There was a small leftover fire smouldering in the fireplace. She got up and went to stand there, feeling the sudden warmth on her legs. She looked up to the mantel, where there was a cup filled with feathers. The feathers, Cassie observed, did not belong to chickadees or goldfinches or any other birds that Cassie knew of. She frowned and turned around.

"She must be shedding," said Cassie curtly. "She's losing all her feathers."

The writer smiled. "Molting, I think the word is," he said, looking thoughtful. "Actually, I would prefer to call it emerging."

"Emerging?" asked Cassie.

The writer poured the tea into two cups and

nodded, leaning back in his writing chair, looking for all the world as if he knew everything. Cassie sat down and put her hands around the warm teacup.

"We all"—he peered at Cassie—"you, too, do a lot of emerging. Like butterflies. Like moths from cocoons. Sometimes we don't even know we're doing it."

"How can we do that?" asked Cassie, spooning a fifth teaspoon of sugar into her tea that was too strong. "I mean without knowing it."

The writer drank some tea, making a loud slurping noise, and they laughed.

"Well, you emerged from babyhood into childhood hardly even thinking about it, didn't you?" he asked.

Cassie thought a moment. "That's true, I guess," she said slowly. "I did run away once," she added.

He nodded. "Me, too. When I was a child, that is. It gets a bit harder to run away when you're older. So sometimes we build cocoons around us and linger inside awhile."

Cassie leaned back in her chair and thought about her tablecloth and the door under the back stairs and being up in trees looking down. She remembered her mother's words to Coralinda when Cassie had hidden. There was something here she didn't understand but almost did. Like remembering only half of a joke or only the begin-

78

ning of a story. And it all had to do with feathers and wearing hats and saying rhymes. And hiding, and inside and outside. And emerging.

"Why is it," said Cassie, peering over her teacup, "that I like to hear what you say even though I don't understand what you're saying at all?"

The writer laughed, and so did Cassie. And the two of them sat and sipped terrible tea in silence until the sun had slipped down past the dunes.

12

Catching Snow

"HAVE YOU EVER BEEN IN LOVE, Margaret Mary?" asked Cassie. She never took her eyes off the rowboat in the inlet and the two figures in the boat.

"Certainly," said Margaret Mary. She slurped a sour ball, moving it from one cheek to the other.

The one rowing the boat was not paying attention, and the boat jigged back and forth in a half-hearted way. It might have been funny if it had been anyone other than the writer rowing with Cousin Coralinda.

"I thought he was supposed to be writing," Cassie muttered grumpily.

Margaret Mary looked quickly at Cassie, then back out to the boat.

"The first time I was in love," she began, "was with Timothy Farquat-Sperry. Imagine! Margaret Mary Farquat-Sperry! I think it was his name I loved. And of course his yo-yo that glowed in the dark."

"Well, I've never loved anyone 'til now," said Cassie, crossing her fingers behind her back because she'd suddenly remembered Mr. Bagg.

Margaret Mary sighed. "You'd best be careful," she said wisely. "I once read my Aunt Cecily's romance magazines. They were full of pain and anguish."

"Anguish?" said Cassie, studying the bulge in Margaret Mary's right cheek. "What's anguish?"

"Like pain, I think," said Margaret Mary, "but seven times worse. I remember best 'Teens in Trouble.' It was packed with anguish." Margaret Mary smiled. "My mum says that the only thing worse than a teen in trouble is more than one teen in trouble."

Cassie laughed. "Your mom said that?" Cassie was surprised. "Your mom doesn't seem the type to say that."

"Well," said Margaret Mary, getting up and

brushing sand from her pants and shirt, "there are many surprises in life. Nothing is much like it first appears."

"Yes," said Cassie, putting her chin in her hand and looking out at the rowboat, "I know."

She watched the rowboat for a long time, long after Margaret Mary had gone home to check her mother's slop sauce, simmering on the stove. Finally, shaking her head as if shaking away any anguish that might be lurking there, she went to find her mother.

Cassie found a paint scraper and helped her mother scrape around the windows of the cottage nearest the inlet. It was hard work. But worse than hard work, Cassie could still see the reflection of the rowboat in the window glass.

"Why are we working so hard on these cottages anyway?" she asked in a loud voice. "The renters will probably be loud and have naked parties."

Cassie's mother laughed.

"That might be nice," she said, teasing, putting her hand on Cassie's cheek. She picked up the hedge clippers and began cutting back the sumac that grew close to the cottage.

Cassie watched her mother. She remembered when late one night her mother and father ran down to the sea with no clothes on. They swam, and when they came from the water, their bodies glistening like seals in the moonlight, they had put their arms around each other. It wasn't proper, thought Cassie, not for them, not for any passing fisherman to see, much less for their very own daughter with her nose pressed against the window glass, watching.

Gran came into the yard, carrying a wooden box and an easel, steering Baby Binnie in front of her. Binnie walked precariously on tiptoes, first one way, then the other, like a drunk dancer. Suddenly she sat down hard with a surprised look on her face.

Cassie got down from the small stepladder and sat in front of Binnie.

"Say Cass," she whispered. "Please. Say Cass."

"Poodee," said Baby Binnie, deciding not to cry about sitting down hard. She smiled broadly at Cassie.

Gran unloaded the box and easel.

"Today I'm going to start painting," she said.

Cassie peered into the box. "You mean a picture?" said Cassie. "What are you going to paint?"

"Don't know yet."

"Don't know! You have to know what you're going to paint before you paint it," insisted Cassie.

"Now who made that rule?" asked Gran. "That's downright boring."

"Well, make it something beautiful," said Cassie

grumpily. "I'm tired of all this." She stared out at the dunes and the sea.

Gran sighed. "I just wish I could make it like 'all of this.'"

Cassie stared at Gran.

"How come you don't see things the way they are?" she asked.

Gran straightened up from her paint box. "My fault, eh Cassie? Tell me, just how are things? How *are* things?"

A sudden picture of James flashed through Cassie's head. She remembered a long time ago—or was it just a week or two?—James standing in front of the dark kitchen window and asking Cassie, "And what is everyone else like, Cass?" She had had no answers for James then. And now she had no answer for Gran. She thought about the question and answer sheet in the upstairs bathroom. No answers anywhere, thought Cassie. And suddenly, because there seemed to be nothing left to do, Cassie surprised herself by bursting into tears. Gran looked up, her eyebrows arched, as Cassie leaned her face against a tree. After a moment, Gran put down her paint box and turned Cassie around, taking her in her arms.

"Dear Cass," murmured Gran. "Don't you know, child, that everyone has a different way of looking at things? It's as if we all have eyeglasses to look through—eyeglasses of our own." Gran pulled back a bit and looked down at Cassie. "Now Binnie there . . ." Baby Binnie, hearing her name, looked up and smiled at Gran. "She's too young to look through anyone else's glasses. But you, Cass, are growing up. Learning how to look through other people's eyeglasses. Do you see?"

Cassie shook her head.

"I don't know. I'm not sure."

"Of course not," said Gran. "You don't have to be sure. It's not easy, this learning to see the world the way others see it. Some grown-ups never learn." She looked at Cassie, hesitating. "Papa never learned it."

"Papa!" Cassie took a step backward. "But Papa was perfect!"

"Perfect?" Gran smiled. "Never perfect, Cassie. There were moments of being perfect, perhaps. Moments for us all. But never perfect all the time, thank goodness."

The old memory was there again in front of Cassie's eyes. Papa in the bed, calling after Cassie. Cassie yelling at him, stamping her foot.

"Don't you remember, Cass, Papa always wishing for things to be the way he thought they ought to be? Angry, unhappy because they weren't. Don't you remember catching snow with Papa during the first snowfall?"

Cassie pushed the memory away and remembered running outside with Papa, the snow falling

85

densely, Cassie trying to catch the flakes on her mitten. Furious because they wouldn't stay on her hand.

"Remember?" asked Gran. "You wanted them to stay perfect forever."

Cassie nodded, remembering.

"Well, Papa wished for the same," said Gran. "He never learned that most things are only there for a moment, quite perfect and fine, like snow."

Catching snow. Cassie thought about it as she watched Gran open her paint box and set up her easel. Catching snow. She felt a gentle tugging at her shirt, and looked down to see Baby Binnie holding out her arms. Cassie smiled and picked her up, and Binnie put her plump arms around Cassie's neck, hanging on tightly, laying her head on Cassie's shoulder.

"Oh Binnie," whispered Cassie, kissing Binnie's soft ear. "Catching snow. Just what do you think about catching snow, Binnie?"

Baby Binnie sighed and settled closer into Cassie's neck.

"Cass," she answered softly. "Cass."

13

Eyeglasses

THE DAYS OF LATE SUMMER grew shorter and the light changed beneath the tablecloth. It was more dark and confining to Cassie, and she rarely stayed there for long. She paid less attention to conversations, hearing only snatches of talk.

"A storm's coming," she heard her father say. "We'd better keep watch on that."

"Why Cor, you look lovely. New dress? New perfume? New feathers?"

"Fourteen and three/I'll have more tea."

The writer never spoke about his writing. But from time to time he would stretch out a booted foot beneath the tablecloth and touch Cassie. She would smile and imagine him smiling above the table.

Gran worked on her painting daily, sometimes behind the big dune, out of the wind, sometimes behind the house. Once Cassie came upon her on the path to the writer's cottage, working intently.

"No peeks. No looking," she insisted. "It's not ready for lookers yet. Soon."

Cassie was curious. What could she be painting?

"Patience," called the watching writer, sitting on the front steps of his porch.

Cassie smiled. The writer had very little patience himself, and lately the most noticeable sound she heard from his cottage was the wrenching sound of paper being ripped from the typewriter. It was a sound that made Cassie wince.

"Any answers yet?" asked the writer, smiling back at her. Cassie noticed that one of his front teeth was slightly crooked. Funny that she'd never noticed that before.

"Only some," Cassie answered. "Only some."

"Well, you can't ask for more than that, can you?" he said.

"Yes I can," said Cassie stubbornly, making him laugh.

"Growing up," said the writer, sounding like a very old man, "is a rough business. I remember someone once saying that it was like pedaling furiously, but only going backward."

Cassie smiled. "Gran says growing up is putting on different eyeglasses to look at life."

"Ah." The writer liked that. "Your Gran is wise." He peered at Cassie. "You know, you're very much like your Gran."

Like Gran? Cassie was astonished. He nodded. "And you'll be more like her when you stop hiding," he added. "I saw you up the tree again yesterday."

Cassie's face grew hot. To get back at him, she decided to ask about his writing. She had seen his light burning late the night before, and noticed the dark circles under his eyes.

"What are you writing?"

He frowned. "A short story."

"That must be easier to write than a novel. Shorter. Smaller," said Cassie.

The writer looked at her.

"Is it easier to be a child than an adult?" he asked. "Because you are shorter? Smaller?"

"There you go again," Cassie accused him. "Answering a question with another question!"

"It makes you think," said the writer calmly.

"But I really want to know," said Cassie. "Why do you like to write short stories?"

The writer leaned back against a porch post, long legs stretched out in front of him. "Well, I think a short story is like a poem. A small piece of something, full circle, there for a time, then not there."

"Like catching snow," said Cassie thoughtfully.

"Catching snow?"

Cassie nodded. "Gran says that life is filled with small perfect moments that are only there for a short time. And then gone. Like catching snow on your hand."

The writer smiled. "Catching snow," he murmured.

"What do you think?" asked Cassie.

"I think," said the writer, "that catching snow is wonderful." He grinned at her. "Just wonderful."

"Well, at least you answered *that* question," said Cassie, smiling back at him. She ran off to visit Uncle Hat, looking back only once to see the writer looking after her, still smiling.

Uncle Hat sat out on the hill with his telescope, watching a flock of birds on the water. His orange hat looked fluorescent, and Cassie watched him for a while before climbing up to sit next to him.

"What do you see?" she asked, shading her eyes, looking at the small dots bobbing on the water.

Uncle Hat didn't answer.

Cassie looked sideways and smiled. All right, she'd play his game.

"Four and three/What do you see?" she asked.

"Cormorants," said Hat promptly. "Out there. See, there's one on the rock, standing with his wings out." He moved so Cassie could look through the scope.

"I've never seen those before!" exclaimed Cassie indignantly. She watched a long-necked dark bird stand, beak up, to air out its wings.

"Maybe you never looked before," said Hat.

Cassie looked quickly at him, but he was peering into the scope again, moving it slowly, scanning the sea.

"Hat?"

"Yo."

"What do you know about catching snow?"

"Not too much," said Hat, staring into the scope. "Mostly I know about counting birds. They're there. Then they're not there."

"But that's like catching snow!" cried Cassie, grinning at him.

"'S'at so," commented Hat, not looking at her.

There was a long silence.

"Hat? How come you never showed me those birds before?"

"Never asked," said Hat. He turned his head to look at Cassie. "People who don't ask questions usually think they got things all figured out. They think they know all the answers."

Cassie, stung a bit, moved down from the hill and stood up.

"You're not talking in rhymes," she accused him.

"Nope," said Hat, smiling at Cassie. "Sometimes I don't have to."

Cassie turned to leave, then heard his thin voice call after her.

"Everyone has his own way of hiding, Cassie. Twelve and two/The same with you."

Margaret Mary had covered herself, all except her head, in sand.

"Terribly glad you're here, Cass," she said, looking up at Cassie. "I'm about to depart this world, but before I do I wish to say good-bye to a good friend, Cassandra Binegar, and will her my favorite rosemary plant, named Hair Ball."

Cassie laughed. Margaret Mary named everything. She had once named a bandage she'd worn on her toe for a week. She probably even named her socks.

"Any last words before I cover my face with sand?"

Cassie sat down next to Margaret Mary's sand body.

"Margaret Mary, have you ever caught snow?"

Margaret Mary squinted her eyes, looking thoughtful. "Never seen much snow, actually." She moved her arms back and forth through the sand, making angels. "But in England we have lots of fog. Does fog count, Cass?" Margaret Mary stood up, the sand falling away from her like water, and they began walking up the dunes to Margaret Mary's house.

Cassie thought about fog. It came from somewhere, going nowhere. Like snow. Cassie stopped and turned around abruptly with a new thought. Like the sea!

"I don't know," she said, gazing out over the dunes and the water. "But I am willing to bet, Margaret Mary, that fog counts."

Looking through the eyeglasses of others, thought Cassie. She thought of her father, running from a taxi through the crowds to buy violets. She thought of Uncle Hat, sometimes rhyming, sometimes not. Coralinda wearing feathers, but changing before her eyes, becoming beautiful.

They reached Margaret Mary's yard, Cassie trailing her fingers along the leaves of the privet hedge. She noticed that Margaret Mary's mother had not yet won her battle with the wild honeysuckle, the shoots beginning to tangle around the bottom of the hedge. At the front door, Margaret Mary bent down to pull at some weeds around bright flowers.

"Margaret Mary!" Cassie knelt, touching the flowers. "These flowers are real!"

Margaret Mary grinned at Cassie.

"Marigolds," she said proudly. "I grew them from seeds."

"But why?" asked Cassie.

Margaret Mary knelt beside her. She sat back on her heels and looked at her plants.

"Well," she began, "they grow, for one thing. They'll grow and fill in all the spaces here. And they'll change. New blooms. They won't always look the same."

Cassie and Margaret Mary stared at each other for a moment, then Cassie smiled.

"Splendid," she announced, sounding just like Margaret Mary. "That's splendid."

She left Margaret Mary, happily weeding, and went inside Margaret Mary's house to wash her hands. The bathroom was dark and quiet and clean and perfect. Smiling at herself in the mirror, Cassie washed her hands, leaving a slight smudge of dirt on the white porcelain. She did not rinse it off. She opened the clothes hamper and draped the bottom half of a pair of men's pajamas over the side.

"It's only the outside," she whispered, echoing Margaret Mary's words from a long time ago. Then she shut the door firmly and went outside to think about fog and snow and the sea.

14

The Lavender Dress

THE SKY WAS STARLESS when Cassie went to bed, and during the night the wind rose. A shutter banged against the house, waking Cassie, and she lay in bed, eyes open, listening to the roar of the waves beyond the inlet. At last she slept, and when she woke she could see morning light around the edges of the window shade. She heard the noises of her family downstairs and she got up, pulling her old blue corduroy robe around her, and went down to the kitchen.

"Cassie!" Her father reached out for her and pulled her close, pushing her nose into his flannel

95

shirt. "Why up so early? It's no good of a day."

Cassie untangled herself from her father's arms and the smells of his pipe and the hall closet.

"Are you fishing today?" Cassie peered out the window anxiously. "It's too stormy."

James looked up from a tangle of lines and smiled at her.

"It's nice," he answered. "Just right."

Cassie sighed and sat down as John Thomas rumpled her hair. She watched her mother pour coffee into her father's thermos. She wore her husband's nightshirt and she looked like a colt, mostly long tan legs and unbrushed hair like a mane.

"Is your lunch packed?" Cassie's mother smiled at Cassie's father. In answer, he pulled her close and they kissed. Cassie used to frown when they kissed, or count how long each kiss lasted, but suddenly she caught James's eye and they smiled at each other across the table.

"You know, Cass, I almost forgot," said James, searching through his bait box. "I have something for you. From down under."

Cassie smiled. Down under. How many times had James found treasures from the sea. Down under, he called it. Once a brass buckle, green from the sea. Another time an old black pointed shoe from long ago, so soft that the leather fell away from the shoe when it was touched.

"Look. Here it is," James called softly, his hand

held out. "It's for you. Good luck."

Cassie moved closer to James and looked at what he held in his hand. It was a small gold ring, the carving on the sides worn smooth by the water. Cassie turned it over in her hand, and the light from the lamp caught the gold.

"Guess how it came up?" whispered James.

"How?"

"In some seaweed tangled in a lobster pot," said James, smiling. "Do you suppose the lobster was married?"

Cassie turned the ring over, pausing for a moment, as always, to mourn for the lobster who would be someone's dinner. She sighed, and put the ring on her smallest finger. It fit perfectly.

"A good luck sign from the sea for Cassie Binegar," said James, looking pleased. "From down under."

Cassie frowned. "But what about you? Maybe it was a sign for you, James?" She looked up to see James shaking his head.

"No, Cass. The ring fits you. It's yours. I'll find something else for good luck."

Cassie knew almost all fishermen had good luck pieces. John Thomas carried an old coin in his pocket. Cassie's father carried a leather pouch with a lock of his wife's hair. One old fisherman had always taken his small dog fishing. When the dog had died, peacefully, of old age and many hours at sea, the fisherman had never fished again.

"Come," Cassie's father called to her brothers. "It's getting late."

James picked up the metal box; John Thomas carried extra line. Cassie looked down at the ring on her finger. Then she looked out at the sea, the gray now curling with white caps.

"Wait!" Her brothers and her father turned at the door. "Don't go."

Her father smiled. "Hey, Cass. We've been out in worse."

The wind came in a rush with the rain, and they turned to run to the truck.

"Wait." Cassie's hand found the old doll, the girl doll, in her pocket. She took it out and handed it to James.

"Good luck sign. For you," she said.

James smiled, turning it over in his hand, then putting it in his pocket. "Cassie Binegar goes to sea," he said, reaching out to hug her. She didn't pull away.

They left then, the door closing with a sudden rush of the wind, leaving Cassie and her mother in the kitchen. Cassie's mother went to the window and watched as the truck started up and wound its way down the hill. Cassie leaned against the kitchen door and watched her mother, noticing for the first time the small lines on her forehead, on the sides of her mouth. *She worries too,* thought Cassie suddenly. Her mother stood on tiptoes, following the truck with her eyes.

She waved, a short quick movement, then turned and smiled self-consciously when she saw Cassie.

"They never see me wave," she explained. "But I do it every day anyway."

Cassie nodded. "I didn't know you worried. It doesn't show."

"I guess, Cass, that's because you can't see what goes on inside my head." She put her arm around Cassie. "It's private."

Private. Something stirred inside Cassie. Something to remember. To take note of. Cassie walked upstairs to dress. Private. Inside my head. Cassie walked into the bathroom and read the writing on the sheet.

> Each of us has a space of his own. We carry it around as close as skin, as private as our dreams. What makes you think you don't have your own, too?

Cassie grinned suddenly. She picked up the pencil and wrote.

> I do have my own space.

Then underneath Cassie drew a small picture, rather rough but still recognizable. She leaned back and smiled at it as if it were a masterpiece. It was a pair of eyeglasses.

"Gran."

Cassie had gone to the attic to look for the kaleidoscope. And there was Gran, going through a trunk of clothes, her hair in a tumbled cloud around her head.

"What are you looking for?" asked Cassie, settling by Gran.

Gran sat back. "A dress. A lavender dress. I need it for my painting. Want to help?"

"What kind of dress?" asked Cassie. The rain blew in a sudden burst against the attic roof, the sound loud and menacing. Gran and Cassie looked at each other.

"Where's your mother?"

"Gone to check for roof leaks on the cottages," said Cassie. "What kind of dress?" she repeated.

"Special," said Gran, smiling mysteriously. "Look, here's your kaleidoscope." She handed it to Cassie. "Ah, here it is." Gran bent down and picked up a large box. Slowly, she took off the cover and parted the yellowed tissue paper inside. She stared at it for so long that Cassie finally leaned over and looked in.

"Lavender," said Cassie softly. Lavender, the same color as the doll in Cassie's dollhouse.

"My wedding dress," said Gran. "And your

mother's. Two weddings this dress has seen." She looked at Cassie. "So far." She took it out of the box and stood up, slowly unfolding the dress. She walked over to the long mirror propped in the corner and held it in front of her. It was the soft color of old glass, with a high neck and long sleeves with ivory lace edgings that fell away in folds. It reached Gran's feet.

There was a sound behind Gran and Cassie, and they turned to see Cassie's mother, her hair streaming, her face wet with rain. She smiled.

"You found it. Good." She climbed up the stairs and sat, rolling the long hanks of hair between her hands, trying to dry them. "No leaks, thank goodness."

Gran turned from the mirror. "Do a favor for an old woman," she said to Cassie's mother. "Try it on."

Cassie's mother laughed. "Me? Now, like this?"

"Go on," said Cassie. "Do it. Try it on."

Her mother shrugged and got up, stripping off her rain gear and her wet sweater and jeans. Shivering a bit in the attic cold, she stood, while Gran settled the dress over her head, zipping up the back.

"There," said Gran. "Now, turn around."

She shouldn't have looked so beautiful, thought Cassie, with only the bare light overhead and her hair still wet and beginning to curl. But she did.

She looked like a mermaid, come from the sea to try on a human dress. *Whose eyeglasses am I looking through now?* thought Cassie, as the three of them—Gran, Cassie's mother, and Cassie—stood as if enchanted by a long lavender dress.

15

The Storm

DOWN FROM THE ATTIC, Cassie looked out the
windows, watching Gran carry the carefully plastic-
wrapped dress to her cottage. Cassie had thought
the sky couldn't grow darker, but it had. The sand
blew and there were no birds flying.

"Where are the birds?" Cassie whispered to
Hat. He stood at the kitchen window in his foul-
weather gear, jacket and pants, a blue knitted hat
under his rain hood.

"Taken cover," he said, looking through the
binoculars. "When the wind is this bad the birds
find somewhere safe."

103

"Do you see any boats?" asked Cassie, straining to see.

"No boats," answered Hat. Then he looked down at her. "Cass, are you worried? About your brothers and your father?"

"No," said Cassie. "Yes," she said softly. She was worried. The memory of Papa in the bed, calling to her, had intruded all day. Why was it here now? She had, at last, done the right thing. She had given the doll to James for good luck. To keep him safe. To keep things from changing. Even though she had not told Papa she was sorry about yelling, she had given James the doll. Didn't that make up for it at all?

The door blew open, Cousin Coralinda and the writer grabbing it. They stood dripping by the kitchen door, catching their breath. Slowly, the writer unwrapped Baby Binnie from under his poncho. Cousin Coralinda took off Binnie's hat and sweater.

"Will you watch her, Cass?" Coralinda asked, breathless from running. "We've got to find the rowboat and pull it up."

"The tide's running high," said the writer, looking worried.

"I'll come, too," said Hat, handing his binoculars to Cassie. "Be back."

Cassie smiled at Binnie, who after a brief look around began to unravel one corner of the rag

104

rug. Cassie went to the window, peering out through the storm. Gran came up the driveway, her head bent low. Cassie saw her stop, only for a moment, and pick something up from the mud. Then she came up the steps and into the kitchen.

"Hi, Binnie dear." Gran blew a kiss to Binnie and Binnie kissed her own hand in answer.

"Gran, isn't it getting worse?" asked Cassie, watching Gran take off her raincoat and hat.

"It's about the same, I think," said Gran. "Just about the same. Here. Isn't this yours, Cass?" Gran held out her hand. And there, small and mud covered and soggy with rain, lay the small doll from Cassie's dollhouse.

The doll.

"No!" cried Cassie. "I gave it to James. Why doesn't he have it?"

"Cass. What is it? What is the matter?" Gran put her arm around Cassie, but Cassie pulled away.

"It's just the same!" she shouted, beginning to cry. "I should have told Papa I was sorry I yelled. Maybe he'd be alive now. And now James! He'll have bad luck!"

"Cass!" Gran spoke sharply. "I don't know what you're talking about."

"Because of me!" shouted Cassie. "It'll be just like Papa. My fault for not doing the right thing. I yelled!" Cassie stopped suddenly and looked at Gran. "Just like now! I'm yelling at you!"

Cassie put her hand over her mouth, staring at Gran. Then she grabbed her raincoat, hanging by the door. She nearly ripped it from its hook as she ran outside.

"Cass!" shouted her Gran.

But Cassie slammed the door behind her, the wind whipping her hair against her face. She ran down the steps and, pausing a moment, scrambled under the porch between the broken slats. She lay in the dry sand in the darkness, crying.

"Cass." A hand pushed her. Her Gran's hand. "Move over. Now!" Gran said sharply.

"Go away!" shouted Cassie.

But Gran crawled under, pulling Binnie with her, wide-eyed, wrapped in a large raincoat.

"Now, what is this." Gran sat Binnie up in the sand. Binnie looked overhead and around. "What about Papa? And yelling?"

The wind had died a bit, and Gran's voice sounded loud in Cassie's ear.

"I yelled at him," Cassie cried, rubbing her eyes now filled with tears and sand. "I didn't say I was sorry." She looked up at Gran. "And he died." The words, the first time ever spoken by Cassie, seemed to fill the place beneath the porch.

"So," said Gran, taking out her handkerchief and rubbing Cassie's eyes. "So you yelled. And Papa yelled. Yes?"

Cassie looked up. "I don't know. I don't remember if Papa yelled." She began to cry again. "It doesn't matter."

"Then why does it matter that you yelled?" Gran's voice was soft and sad.

Cassie sat up. "I don't know. I don't know anything."

Gran pulled Cassie close to her.

"And you kept this to yourself all this time? Cass, that makes it so much harder for you. Don't you know that?" Gran sighed. "I'll tell you something, Cass. Papa died because he was sick. And Papa yelled, too. He yelled just before he died, Cass. He sat up in bed and yelled 'Where in hell are my green socks!' Then he died. That was all."

Cassie stared at Gran. Gran smiled, and they began to laugh and cry at the same time, holding on to each other, Baby Binnie watching them.

"You've got to let it go, Cass," whispered Gran. "You know, after Papa died I came on a footprint of his in the garden. It was so perfect, so clear, just as if he'd passed that way a moment before. I would go out and look at it, day after day. Once I even put a wooden carton over it so it would stay. But it didn't. The rain began to wash it away, slowly, and one day it wasn't there anymore."

There was silence.

"Like catching snow," said Cassie in Gran's ear.

Gran nodded. "Yes, like catching snow."

It was quiet then. Baby Binnie, staring solemnly

at Cassie and Gran, reached over to touch a tear on Gran's cheek. But she said nothing. The wind and rain had died. The storm was gone. And the only sound was the dripping of water off the roof to the porch below.

16

Birds Across the Moon

THE AFTERNOON WAS CLEAR and sharp. "It's always this way after a storm," Cassie's father told Cassie and Margaret Mary on the porch, later when all the scenes of the day had flickered out. Cassie smiled at him, then lifted her face to smell the clean smells of earth and rain. The scent of roses hung about, though the flowers on her mother's rosebush lay on the ground, stripped from the limbs by the rain. Everything smelled different to Cassie. When she and her mother had driven to the fish pier to watch for her father's boat, the old wood planks of the wharf had smelled sweet and new. When the boat came, Cassie and her mother watching excitedly through binoculars, the boat had not smelled of fish to Cassie. Or if it had, Cassie had not noticed. She didn't wrinkle her nose or frown. "It should be decorated," she remembered saying. "It brought them back." And she had stared at the boat, shining and beautiful in the late afternoon light.

When they returned in the truck, Uncle Hat had run down the hill to greet them, followed by Bumble Bee who thought it was a game. Hat was, for the first time Cassie could ever remember, hatless, and his rain hood flopped behind him.

"Uncle Hat!" Cassie had blurted when the truck stopped. "You've got hair!"

Hat had stopped to smile at Cassie. "So've you," he had announced. "And so have you," he'd said to James. "And you. And you!"

Cassie grinned. She might never know just why Hat wore hats or spoke in rhymes sometimes. But it didn't matter anymore. It wasn't important. Cassie put her hand in her jacket pocket and took out the doll, now grimy with dried mud. Silently, she reached out and gave it to James.

"Ah." James turned the doll over in his hand. "I wondered where it was."

Cassie reached out to brush some of the dried mud away. "Gran found it," she said. "Outside."

Smiling, James put the doll in his jacket pocket and buttoned the pocket.

"Cassie Binegar had a hard day of it," he said, his hand lingering over the pocket for a moment. "But," he added softly, "she weathered the storm."

Inside the house, Gran had made hot tea, and Coralinda had baked things that resembled biscuits. Baby Binnie had thrown one across the room in a sudden burst of energy, and it had bounced and skidded along the floor.

"They are wonderful," the writer had murmured, managing to look adoring while trying to bite into one. "Really, Cor."

Cor. His soft voice wrapped itself around the name. Cassie and Margaret Mary had looked at each other, then Cassie had sighed and leaned over to her Gran.

"I suppose," she whispered, "this means no more pain and anguish for Cousin Coralinda. They'll probably get married and swim naked in the sea."

Gran had looked at Cassie for a moment. She had not laughed, but had reached over to take Cassie's hand and to whisper back, "Oh, dear Cass, I do believe you are right."

Margaret Mary, sitting on the other side of Gran, leaned over. "I've seen it coming, too. I ran across

111

them, clapped quite close together, kissing in the pathway day before yesterday."

"I hope," said Cassie, frowning, "that it doesn't interfere with his writing."

Gran smiled broadly at Cassie. "It may help," she said, staring straight ahead again as if they had not been talking at all.

After dinner, when it was dark, they sat quietly on the half-lighted porch. James and John Thomas had gone to bed, weary from a hard day at sea. Cassie's mother and father had gone swimming wearing their bathing suits. Cousin Coralinda and the writer were inside, gazing at each other over cold cups of tea. Uncle Hat, looking through his telescope, was counting birds as they passed the moon while Baby Binnie sat close behind him, making buildings out of pots and pans. They would fall, from time to time, the clatter making Gran and Margaret Mary and Cassie jump. But Uncle Hat counted on. "One hundred and seventy-two, seventy-three, seventy-four and five . . ."

"School starts soon," said Margaret Mary, leaning back in her chair. "Won't it be sad to have the summer over?"

"Seventy-seven, seventy-eight . . ."

"There's always next summer," said Cassie. "New people to meet. New things happening."

She turned to Gran with a sudden thought. "That's what Papa told me."

Gran nodded.

"Eighty-three, one hundred and eighty-four," Uncle Hat went on.

"I've got something for you, Gran," Cassie said suddenly. "But right now it's in my head. Not finished yet."

Gran smiled and slowly got up.

"I've got something for *you*." She walked inside the house. "And not in my head," she called.

"Eighty-seven, eighty-eight . . ."

The building fell, and Baby Binnie grinned.

Cassie and Margaret Mary looked up as Gran stood there.

"The painting!" Cassie got up quickly.

"Remember," said Gran, "you said to paint something beautiful. And I did. It's for you." She handed the painting to Cassie.

The painting was not of the sea or the dunes or a bush of sea roses as Cassie had thought it might be. It was a woman, seated, her hair swept up on her head. She was wearing the lavender dress.

"Is it you?" Margaret Mary asked Gran. "You in your wedding dress?" She looked closer. "Or Cassie's mum?"

"No," said Cassie, her voice sounding breathless

113

to her. She looked more closely at the painting. On the smallest finger of the woman's right hand was a small gold ring. The ring from down under. Cassie looked at Gran. "It's me, isn't it?"

Gran put her arm around Cassie. "It is Cassie Binegar," she said smiling at Cassie.

Cassie shook her head slowly. "It's beautiful, Gran. It really is."

"I wanted to paint you in the wedding dress, Cass," said Gran softly. "I may never get to see you at your own wedding, you know."

"Eighty-nine, ninety, one hundred and ninety-one, one hundred and ninety-two . . ." Hat's voice was clear in the still night. Cassie looked at him, then back at Gran.

"Gran," she began, handing the picture back to her. "I think you should have it. For a while, at least. Later it can be mine."

Gran smiled. "Looking through my eyeglasses, now, aren't you Cassie?" She went inside, putting the painting on the mantel, standing to look at it for a moment.

"Drat," said Uncle Hat, staring through the scope. "Two more just flew by. Where did I leave off?"

Baby Binnie's building of pots and pans fell, and she looked up. "One hundred and ninety-two," she announced, putting a small finger in her ear.

"What?!" Cassie and Margaret Mary began laughing.

"Say it again, Binnie," said Cassie.

"Say one hundred and ninety-two," pleaded Margaret Mary.

Baby Binnie looked up at them and silently began rebuilding her tower.

"She won't say it again!" exclaimed Margaret Mary. "Only once. It's almost as if we dreamed it, isn't it? Like catching fog, didn't you say?"

"Snow, Margaret Mary," said Cassie softly as she looked up to see Gran standing in the doorway, the light behind her. "Like catching snow."

"Ah," said Uncle Hat, smiling, still staring through his telescope, "we're old friends, aren't we, Binnie?"

"Murp," answered Baby Binnie, nodding her head up and down, smiling up at Uncle Hat.

Cassie dreamed of a hermit crab, scuttling through the sands of her sleep. She awoke in the dark, smiling. There was no dream of Papa. She knew that dream would not come again. She turned on the light, got up, and opened the drawer of her dresser. She searched through the tumble of socks and underwear and notebooks until she found the tissue-wrapped grandfather doll. Carefully she unwrapped it, smoothing the white shirt. She walked up the attic stairs, quietly, so as not to wake anyone. The old dollhouse sat in a corner of the attic, behind the boxes and suitcases of Cassie's life before. All the dolls lived within; the mother, the father, the brothers, the grandmother. Cassie put out one finger and softly touched the gray hair of the grandfather doll. Then she put him in the house with the others. She thought of the girl doll who lived in James's pocket. "It's the same as being here," she said, her voice like a whisper in the attic.

She found her notebook and sat by the old round window, watching the moon over the stretch of sand and sea before her. She read her poem "Spaces." And then she wrote:

For Gran:
But my very favorite space,
  Behind my nose,
  Behind my face,
    Above my ears
    And past my tears,
      Way in and back beyond my eyes
      Where I sort out my thoughts and sighs
                    and shouts!
                    and cries,

That is where I like to be
Because I know that's really me.

THE END Cassie wrote in small letters under the poem. She stared at it a bit, wrinkling her

116

brow, tilting her head to look at the paper. She shook her head suddenly. And she crossed out THE END, crossing out each letter carefully, and wrote instead: THE BEGINNING.

Very quietly she left the attic. No one but Cassie heard the soft final click of the attic door.

Coralinda Wills, née Binegar, bearing a plethora of nasturtiums, sea roses, marigolds, and plastic leaves intertwined with rosemary sprays lovingly picked by Margaret Mary Brindle, friend of all present, married Jason Thomas Moreau on the shores of Snow Shore on September 22 at sunrise. The bride was preceded by her daughter, Belinda, who strewed, tossed, and pitched rose petals. The bride was accompanied by her maid of honor, Cassandra Kate Binegar, who wore a lavender-and-lace dress worn by her mother on her wedding day as well as by her grandmother, Mrs. Morris Blythe. The bride wore a dotted-swiss dress decorated with feathers.

The bride was given in marriage by her father, Hatfield Binegar, who also presented the wedding party with a poem composed for the occasion entitled "Nine twenty-two/Much Joy for You."

Judge Bender performed the ceremony in the company of family, friends, and sandpipers. Katherine Binegar, cousin of the bride, played a flute processional. Best man John Thomas Binegar and usher James Binegar led those present in the round *"Dona Nobis Pacem."*

The wedding breakfast, consisting of nearly ripe cantaloupe and eggs over, was served on the porch of the Binegar home amidst much laughter and some tears. Afternoon activities included music, swimming, and a pleasant bay ride in the Binegar fishing vessel, named the *Cassandra-Kate.* The boat was decorated for the wedding by the owner, Brendan Binegar, and his daughter, Cassandra. Some members of the wedding party fished unsuccessfully, though it is reported that Mrs. Morris Blythe caught a seven-pound cod.

The groom, newly appointed managing editor of the *Barnstable Recorder*, is also a writer of fiction. His first short story, entitled "Catching Snow," will appear in the April issue of *Pacific Magazine*.

The bride wishes to acknowledge the kindness and forethought and care of all the Binegar family and friends. The groom wishes to thank the family for making it possible for him to meet and love and marry the bride.

3.1 1.0pt.

DATE DUE

OCT 2 3	MAY 16 '7		
JAN 2 2	MAY 25 '9		
MAR 0 4			
OCT 0 8			
NOV 0 2			
JAN 29 '0			
FEB 3 '0			
FEB 9 '0			
APR 7 '0			
APR 20 '0			
APR 21 '0			

Yikes! Grandma's a Teenager

By Dan Greenburg

Illustrated by Jack E. Davis

GROSSET & DUNLAP • NEW YORK

I'd like to thank my editor
Jane O'Connor who makes the process
of writing and revising so much fun,
and without whom
these books would not exist.

I also want to thank Catherine Daly,
Laura Driscoll, and Emily Neye
for their terrific ideas.

Text copyright © 1999 by Dan Greenburg. Illustrations copyright © 1999 by Jack E. Davis.
All rights reserved. Published by Grosset & Dunlap, a member of Penguin Putnam Books
for Young Readers, New York. THE ZACK FILES is a trademark of The Putnam & Grosset
Group. GROSSET & DUNLAP is a trademark of Grosset & Dunlap, Inc. Published
simultaneously in Canada. Printed in the U.S.A.

Library of Congress Cataloging-in-Publication data is available.

ISBN 0-448-41999-8   B C D E F G H I J

Chapter 1

Why is it everybody wants to be some age they aren't? Every kid I know wants to be older. Every grown-up I know wants to be younger. That kills me, boy. Why would anybody want to be younger? I mean, I've *been* younger, and it's not so great. And the story I'm about to tell you proves what I'm saying.

Oh, I should say who I am and stuff. My name is Zack. I'm ten and a half, going on eleven. I go to the Horace Hyde–White School for Boys in New York City. My parents are divorced, and I spend half my time with each of them.

It's always when I'm with Dad that something weird happens. Like the time I opened his refrigerator and found a turnip that looked and sang just like Elvis Presley. Or the time Dad took me to this Chinese restaurant and all the fortunes in the fortune cookies started coming true. Or the time Dad and I found a UFO in the park and saved a space creature's life.

Or like this time I'm going to tell you about with my Grandma Leah.

Grandma Leah is my dad's mom. She's eighty-eight years old. She lives in Chicago, where my dad grew up. When my grandma was a girl in Poland, she was this really terrific dancer. Then she came to New York. She got a job dancing at Radio City Music Hall as a Rockette.

The Rockettes are a bunch of ladies who

dance in a long line, arm in arm. They kick their legs way up high. They do it at exactly the same time, the way guys in the Army march. I don't mean guys in the Army dance in a long line, kicking their legs up, but you get the idea.

Anyway, Radio City Music Hall was having this big party, a Rockettes Reunion. They found out my grandma was the oldest living Rockette. They asked her to come to New York to be part of the celebration. She would stay for a week. While she was in New York, we'd get to celebrate her eighty-ninth birthday. And she'd come to school for Grandparents Day.

Dad and I went out to the airport to meet Grandma Leah and bring her back to Dad's apartment. Her plane landed. All the people arrived. But no Grandma Leah. Dad was getting worried. Then we heard this *beep-beep*, and there she was. On a little electric cart, driven by a guy in a blue uniform. Grandma Leah looked confused and a little dizzy.

"Grandma!" I said. "Where were you?"

"Mom, we were so worried!" said Dad. "What happened to you?"

"I got lost," she said. "I was looking for the baggage claim. And I somehow ended up where you go to get on other airplanes."

"What happened then?" asked my dad, helping Grandma Leah off the electric cart.

"I was so confused, I went through the metal detector *backwards*. It made loud noises. Sparks shot out. It caused quite a fuss, I tell you. They said it never happened before. I have no idea what I did. I do hope I didn't break their machine."

"Oh, Mom, I doubt that you broke their machine," said Dad. He hugged her again. We picked up Grandma's bags and left.

When we got to Dad's apartment, Grandma Leah unpacked and showed us her old photo album. She had brought it for the Rockettes reunion. There were pictures of Grandma's husband, Grandpa Sam. There were pictures of Great-Grandpa Maurice when he was a person, before he died and came back as a cat. There were pictures of Grandma in some of her Rockettes outfits. She looked so beautiful and happy. I wish I'd known her when she was that young.

She also showed us her Rockettes bracelet. Grandma jangled her wrist in front of me. "I bet I haven't worn this in over fifty years."

The bracelet was copper, with several crystals set into it. One crystal was a milky color; another was green and seemed to glow. One was purple and was kind of tingly to the touch. On the bracelet, in tiny script, was written, "Radio City: Experience the Magic."

"I found it when I was going through all my old stuff," said Grandma Leah. "I thought I'd wear it to the party."

Then Grandma yawned. "You know, I'm still feeling a little woozy. I think I will have some hot tea and then go straight to bed."

And that is just what she did.

"Boy," I said, "that thing at the airport seems to have really upset her. I hope she'll be all right in the morning."

"I bet she'll be fine," Dad said. "All she needs is a good night's sleep."

And Dad was sure right about that. In the morning, Grandma Leah woke up feeling like her old self.

"How do you feel, Mom?" asked my dad.

"I feel like my old self," said my grandma. "In fact, I feel *better* than my old self."

"Wonderful," said my dad. "You know, you do look great, Mom. In fact, you look younger than you have in years."

I took a closer look at Grandma. She did look wonderful. And she did look younger. Lots younger.

"I feel like a woman of seventy," she said.

Dad studied her closely.

"You know," he said, "you even *look* like a woman of seventy. How could that be?"

Grandma Leah walked to the full-length mirror on the bathroom door. She studied her reflection. She was standing up straighter. She had fewer wrinkles on her face. She was wearing a big smile.

"It must be the mattress on the bed," she said. "I had a great night's sleep. And I feel like I'm bursting with energy."

Grandma Leah wasn't kidding. She spent the whole time I was at school cleaning the apartment. She washed all the windows. She wanted to paint all the walls and ceilings, but Dad stopped her.

The next morning, Grandma Leah woke

up feeling even better than she had the day before. And she looked even younger. By dinnertime, a stranger probably would have guessed she was no more than fifty.

"Look at you, Mom!" said Dad as he passed her the chicken. "You look fabulous!"

"Holy guacamole, Grandma!" I said. There were hardly any wrinkles in her face or neck. And her hair was way more brown than gray. "You look almost the same age as Dad!" I said.

"Really?" said Grandma Leah. She rushed from the table to the bathroom mirror. I'd never seen her move so fast. "Oh, no!" she cried. "This is terrible!"

"Huh?" said Dad.

"What?" I said.

"This is terrible!" said Grandma Leah.

"Terrible?" I repeated. "How could it be terrible?"

"It is not natural," she said, "for a woman of eighty-eight—almost eighty-nine —to look this young. It's wrong. It is against the laws of nature."

"Mom," said my dad, "anybody in the world would *kill* to suddenly look years younger."

"Well, I am not anybody in the world," said my grandma. "For me to look so young is...is frightening."

"Frightening?" I said.

"Yes," said Grandma Leah. "We must do something to make me look old again."

"Like what?" I asked.

"Maybe I should try to stay up all night tonight," said Grandma Leah.

Dad and I looked at each other. We both thought my grandma was being a little cuckoo. But we do love her. And we didn't want her to be so upset.

"OK, Mom," said my dad. "Whatever you say."

"Tomorrow is Sunday," said Grandma Leah. "The day of the rehearsal for the Rockettes reunion. Remember?" She pointed to the Rockettes bracelet she had on. "I have to look my best. I mean, I have to look *old*."

"OK," said Dad. "I'll get some coffee brewing. Then let's look in the paper and see what late night movies are on TV. I bet if you stay up all night, you'll have terrible bags under your eyes and look really awful by tomorrow."

"You are a wonderful son," said Grandma Leah.

Dad and I looked at each other again. Something weird was definitely going on. But what?

Chapter 2

Early Sunday morning I was awakened by a scream. I jumped out of bed. I dashed out of my bedroom.

Standing in front of the full-length mirror on the bathroom door was Grandma Leah. Except it wasn't Grandma Leah. It was a teenaged version of Grandma Leah. The only way I knew it was Grandma was that she was wearing Grandma's fuzzy pink slippers, her fluffy pink robe, and her Rockettes bracelet.

"This is...like...*amazing*," she said.

"Grandma?"

"This is...like...totally *awesome*," she said.

She couldn't stop looking at herself in the mirror.

"Grandma, is that really you?" I asked. I sounded like Little Red Riding Hood.

"Of course, dear," she said. She was still staring into the mirror. "But this is so...*cool*."

"Uh...yeah" was all I could think of to say.

"And look at this," she said. She pointed to her chin. "Zits."

I looked. She was right. She had two big pimples on her chin.

Just then, my dad walked into the room. He wasn't wearing his glasses. He was rubbing his eyes from sleep.

"I thought I heard somebody scream," he said. "But maybe I dreamed it. Did somebody scream?"

Then he saw Grandma Leah. He screamed.

"Wh-who are you?" he demanded. I think he knew, though. Which is why he screamed.

"Who *am* I?" Grandma repeated. "*Duh*. Like, hel-*lo*-o. I'm your mother. Who else would I be?"

"But you look like...a teenager."

"Yeah," she giggled. She turned to face him. "Isn't it awesome?"

My dad looked like he was going to pass out or something. He leaned against a wall to keep his balance.

"How did this happen?" he whispered.

Grandma Leah shrugged.

"I wake up," she said, "and I'm like, 'What is *up* with me?' I mean, I felt so,

like, *weird*. You know? Then I pass by the bathroom mirror, and *Whoa*! So then Zack comes in, and he goes, 'Grandma, is that really you?'"

She giggled again.

"Grandma," I said, "I don't get it. Last night you were so upset about getting younger. But being a teenager doesn't seem to bother you at all. How come?"

"It's because last night she still had the good judgment of an adult," Dad whispered. "But now she's a crazy teenager."

"Zack, listen," she said, "I grew up in, like, Poland, OK? I mean, I was a teenager in *Poland*. How boring is *that*? Now I get to be a teenager in *America*. In *New York*, right?"

"Uh...yeah," I said. "I sort of see your point. Sort of."

Grandma went into her room and closed the door.

I turned to see how Dad was doing. He wasn't looking so good.

"Well," I said, "at least she seems happy about it."

"How could my mother have become a teenager?" said my dad. "I don't understand." He kept shaking his head.

Grandma Leah came out of her room. She was completely dressed. She looked weird, though. A teenager in old-lady clothes. She walked to the front door.

"Where are you going?" Dad asked.

"Out," said Grandma.

"Out where?"

"What are you, my father?" she asked.

"No," said Dad, "your son. I just want to know where you're going."

"Shopping," said Grandma. "I have to, like, buy some stuff. You know?"

"What kind of stuff are you going to buy?" Dad asked.

"*Stuff*," said Grandma. "A miniskirt. Some platform shoes. Some cool lipstick. You know? Maybe I can even find a place that does body piercing. I'm thinking of getting, like, a ring in my eyebrow."

"What if I don't think that's such a good idea?" Dad asked.

Grandma put her hands on her hips. She looked annoyed.

"What if you don't think that's such a good *idea*?" Grandma repeated. "Hel-*lo*-o. I'm your *mother*, OK?"

"Today is the Rockettes rehearsal at Radio City Music Hall," Dad said. "At two o'clock."

"So?" said Grandma Leah.

"So," said Dad, "try to be back here by one. And tonight you've got that interview with *Entertainment Weekly* magazine."

Grandma kissed us both good-bye and left.

"Oh, boy," said Dad.

"What?"

"I can't wait for that rehearsal," said Dad. "I can't wait to see what they think of the oldest living Rockette."

Chapter 3

Radio City Music Hall is on Sixth Avenue, at Rockefeller Center. It's one of the biggest theaters in the world. They have this humongous organ. Every Christmas they have this huge Christmas show. The Rockettes dance there and stuff. Thousands of people come to see them.

At two in the afternoon on a day when they don't have a show, Radio City Music Hall is deserted. A guard at the door looked us over.

"May I help you?" the guard asked. He didn't look like he wanted to, though.

"We're here for the rehearsal," said my dad.

"Who are you?" said the guard.

"My mother is the oldest living Rockette," said Dad. He pointed to me. "And this is her grandson."

The guard nodded. Then he looked at my grandma. She was wearing her new clothes. A black miniskirt. Big platform shoes. Black lipstick.

"Who are you, the granddaughter?" he asked.

"No," said Grandma, "I'm—"

"That's exactly who she is," said my dad. "The granddaughter. Can we go in?"

"And where's the old lady?" asked the guard.

"She's...here," said my dad.

"You mean she's already in the theater?"

Dad didn't say yes and he didn't say no.

"She's right here at Radio City Music Hall," said Dad. "So can we go in?"

"I guess so," said the guard.

He opened the door to the theater. We went in.

It was even bigger than I remembered. There were about a million seats. Balconies went up to the ceiling. The ceiling was so high, you could jump off the top balcony in a parachute. You'd probably kill yourself, though, because it wouldn't open in time.

Up on stage were a bunch of people. Some Rockettes in street clothes. Some other people. A man was standing in front of the stage. He wore a baseball cap and was holding a clipboard. I figured he was the director. When he saw us, he walked over.

"Are you in the show?" he asked.

"Yes," said my grandma.

"Good," said the director. "We're almost ready to start." He looked at his clipboard. "Name?"

"I'm Grandma Leah," said my grandma. "I'm, like, the oldest living Rockette?"

The director looked up.

"Who are you, hon, her granddaughter?" he asked.

"No, dude," said Grandma, "I'm *her*. Grandma Leah. Hel-*lo*-o. Read my lips."

The director looked at Dad.

"Will Grandma Leah be arriving soon?" he asked. "Because we really do have to get started here."

"She is telling the truth," said my dad. "She really is my mother. She's been getting younger and younger every day. When she arrived in New York, she looked eighty-eight. The next day she looked seventy. The next day she looked *my* age..."

"And then today she woke up looking like this," I said. "We're not sure why this is happening, sir."

The director looked at me. Then at Dad. Then at Grandma Leah. Then at me.

"I suppose you people think this is a big yuck," he said. "Well, we're very busy here. We don't have time for big yucks. I'd like you to leave now. Either come back with Grandma Leah or don't come back at all."

It was pretty obvious the reporter from *Entertainment Weekly* wasn't going to believe teenaged Grandma Leah was the oldest living Rockette. But she really wanted to do the interview. So Dad called the magazine and said Grandma had this really bad cold, and maybe they could do the interview on the phone. The reporter said fine.

Grandma did the interview from the phone in Dad's study. I listened in on the phone in the kitchen.

"So," said the reporter, "you're the oldest living Rockette. Exactly how old *are* you, ma'am?"

"I'm, you know, eighty-eight," said Grandma Leah. "I'll be eighty-nine, on, like, Tuesday."

"Astounding," said the reporter. "You sound so much younger. If I didn't know better, I'd say you were...oh, at least ten years younger than that."

"Yeah, well," said Grandma Leah, "people do say I sound about seventy-eight."

"So tell me. What was it like at Radio City Music Hall?" said the reporter.

"Well," said Grandma Leah, "I remember that it was so *not* fun. This director goes, 'Are you in the show?' And I'm, like, 'Yes.' So he goes, 'Good, we're almost ready to start.' And he's, like, 'Name?' So I go, 'I'm Grandma Leah. I'm, like, the oldest living Rockette?' So—"

"Wait a minute," said the reporter. "How long ago was this?"

"Like about two o'clock?" said Grandma Leah.

"Two o'clock...*today*," said the reporter.

"Well, *duh*," said Grandma Leah.

"I was hoping for a memory that was more than three hours old," said the reporter.

Chapter 4

The next day was Monday. Grandparents Day.

Dad and I got up early. We were kind of nervous to see what age Grandma was going to be when she woke up. We knew she was awake. We could hear her banging around in her room. Then her door opened, and Grandma walked into the living room.

"Hey, what time is breakfast?" she asked. "I'm, like, starving to death here.

Could I have, like, three chocolate-covered doughnuts and a Coke?"

"Grandma," I said, "you're still a teenager."

"Well, *duh*," said my grandma.

"I mean, I thought you might have gotten even younger," I explained.

"Well, I didn't," said my grandma.

"We don't have chocolate-covered doughnuts and a Coke," said my dad.

"OK," said my grandma. "I'll take, like, Pop Tarts and a Dr. Pepper."

"That's not a healthy breakfast," said Dad.

"Who cares?" said Grandma Leah.

"I do," said Dad. "You're a growing girl."

"I'm eighty-eight and I'm growing *younger*, not older," said Grandma Leah.

"She does have a point there," I said.

Dad sighed and shook his head.

"Tell me, Mom," he said, "is *that* what you're planning to wear to Grandparents Day?"

"What's wrong with this?" said Grandma Leah, looking down at her leopard-print miniskirt.

"Well, I just wondered if you had anything else."

"I could change to my *leather* miniskirt," said Grandma. "And, like, this really cool motorcycle jacket I bought."

"Never mind," said Dad. "What you're wearing is fine."

When we got to my school, a lot of the grandparents were already in my homeroom talking to Mrs. Coleman-Levin. Vernon Manteuffel's were there, and so were Spencer Sharp's. Both Vernon and Spencer had normal-looking grandparents. Not me.

Mrs. Coleman-Levin is not only our homeroom teacher. She is also our science teacher. She had set up a table with food for our guests. There was coffee and tea. There were little tiny sandwiches. There were also cookies and cake and stuff.

Andrew Clancy came over to say hello. He's this guy in my class who's always trying to top me.

"This is my friend Andrew," I said to Dad and Grandma. "Andrew, this is my dad and my Grandma Leah."

Andrew shook hands with Dad, then with Grandma Leah.

"Your grandma looks awful young," said Andrew.

I nodded like it was no big deal.

"Well, my grandparents are even younger than yours," Andrew announced.

"Are they here today?" Dad asked.

"Oh, no," said Andrew. "They couldn't

come. They're playing in a championship Little League game. Grandma's pitching."

Just then Mrs. Coleman-Levin came over to say hello.

"Mrs. Coleman-Levin," I said, "this is my dad and my Grandma Leah."

"Pleased to meet you," she said.

Mrs. Coleman-Levin is pretty cool for an adult. You could tell she was dying of curiosity, though.

"You look remarkably...youthful for your age," said Mrs. Coleman-Levin to my grandma.

"Thanks," said my grandma. "You know, I was, like, a Rockette about sixty years ago."

Mrs. Coleman-Levin smiled and nodded. Then she took me aside. "Zack, might I be witnessing an incredible case of reverse-aging?" she asked.

"Yes, ma'am," I said.

"I thought so," said Mrs. Coleman-Levin. She went back to talk more with Grandma Leah. I saw Grandma showing off her Rockettes bracelet.

"Those are very unusual crystals in that bracelet," said Mrs. Coleman-Levin. "The greenish one in particular. It has a strong electromagnetic field. Natives of Pongo-Pongo believe such crystals have very unusual properties."

Mrs. Coleman-Levin knows all about the weird stuff that has happened to me. Like the time Spencer and I traveled out of our bodies and couldn't get back in again. Or the time I drank disappearing ink and became invisible. So Grandma's appearance did not freak her out.

All the grandparents, however, thought Grandma Leah was my older sister. We tried to explain to them, but they just didn't get it. After a while, we gave up trying.

When everybody arrived, Mrs. Coleman-Levin made a short speech. She welcomed all the grandparents. She asked them to tell about their childhoods. Everybody had pretty interesting stories to tell. I couldn't wait for my grandma to tell about her childhood in Poland. But when I looked over at her, I realized she wasn't even paying attention. She was listening to music on headphones.

"Pssst, Grandma," I whispered.

She didn't hear me. I pulled the headphones away from her ears.

"Grandma, what are you doing?" I whispered.

"Listening to hip-hop," she answered. "This CD is awesome."

"Grandma," I said, "you're embarrassing me."

She shrugged. She put the headphones back on her ears.

I stared at Grandma. This was really beyond weird. This was rude. I mean, I've known my grandma my whole life. What was happening to her? She was acting so immature. I mean, there she was with her black lipstick. And her leopard-print miniskirt. And her black leather motorcycle jacket with all the zippers. The only thing that made me know it was her was the Rockettes bracelet on her wrist.

And then I realized something. Grandma's miniskirt no longer fit her. Neither did her motorcycle jacket. They were both way too big. But this morning, they had fit. And her skin had somehow cleared up. Her zits were gone.

I had an awful feeling that I knew what was going on. Grandma Leah was starting to get younger again, right before my very eyes!

I pulled the headphones away from her ears.

"Grandma," I whispered, "something's

happening to you. I think you're growing younger again."

"I am?" she said. She looked confused.

"Yes," I whispered.

She thought a moment. She frowned.

"Something's wrong with this music, too," she said. Her voice sounded higher than before. She took off her headphones.

"This music is so...stupid," she said.

She got up out of her seat. She wandered over to the food table. And this was while Vernon's grandma was telling a funny story about her first time on a plane. I didn't think Grandma Leah was being too polite. I went over to Dad.

"I'm worried about Grandma," I whispered. "I think she's started getting younger again."

I pointed to Grandma at the food table.

"Her clothes don't seem to fit anymore," he said.

"She's getting smaller," I explained.

Grandma Leah put a bunch of sandwiches and other food on a paper plate and went back to her seat. On the way back, she tripped over one of the kids' backpacks. She didn't fall, but she looked embarrassed.

Steven laughed at her, which was a big mistake. Because Grandma Leah took a sandwich and threw it at him. Steven was shocked. Then he threw the sandwich back at her.

"Food fight!" yelled Vernon. He ran to the table to get food to throw. In less than a second, a major food fight was in progress.

"Vernon! Steven! Andrew! Grandma Leah!" yelled Mrs. Coleman-Levin. "You stop that this instant!"

Everybody froze. Grandma Leah, too. They looked pretty scared. Mrs. Coleman-

Levin can yell really loudly when she wants to.

"Do you want me to send all of you down to the principal's office?" shouted Mrs. Coleman-Levin. "Is that what you want me to do?"

The guys and Grandma Leah all shook their heads.

"I'm ashamed of all of you," said Mrs. Coleman-Levin. "Especially in front of our guests. I'm ashamed of the boys, but they're only ten. You, Grandma Leah, should know better, though. You're an adult."

"Am not," said Grandma Leah.

"Are too," said Mrs. Coleman-Levin.

"Am not," said Grandma Leah.

So Mrs. Coleman-Levin sent my grandma to the principal's office.

Chapter 5

After we left school, we got into a cab.

"I just don't know what to do with you, Mom," said Dad. "Even if you're getting younger and younger, it's not like you to act so…naughty."

"Steven started it," said Grandma Leah.

"But, Mom, you threw the sandwich at him first," said Dad.

"Yeah, but he laughed at me," said Grandma Leah.

Dad just rolled his eyes.

We got out of the cab at a girls' clothing store. Dad wanted to buy stuff that fit my grandma. Her miniskirt and motorcycle jacket were so big she was swimming in them.

"May I help you?" said a saleswoman. She was staring at Grandma in a disapproving way.

"Yes," said my dad. "We need to buy a dress or something to replace what she's wearing."

"You can say *that* again," said the saleswoman.

"Excuse me?" said Dad.

"I'd never let any eight-year-old daughter of *mine* dress like that," said the saleswoman.

"Neither would I," said Dad. "But she was a teenager only this morning. And by the way, she's not my daughter. She's my mother."

"Whatever you say," said the sales-woman.

She went to get some dresses to show us.

"I'm sorry I've been a brat," said Grand-ma Leah. "I'm sorry if I embarrassed you. I really am. I mean it." She was getting all teary-eyed.

Dad sighed.

"That's all right, dear," he said. "You're just going through a difficult phase."

"I know it," said my grandma.

"It's not your fault, Grandma," I said.

"I know it," she said. "Plus which, Steven *did* start it."

"Here's what worries me," I said. "Grandma's getting younger and younger, OK? Pretty soon she'll be about five. And pretty soon after that, she'll become a baby. Then an embryo. And then, unless we do something fast, pretty soon she'll disappear altogether."

Grandma Leah burst into tears.

"Oh, no!" she wailed. "Oh, no-o-o-o-o-o!"

"And if Grandma Leah disappears," I said, "then you'll disappear too, Dad. You'll never have been born. And neither will I."

Dad looked startled. "You're right," he said. "I never thought of it like that."

"We have to do something fast," I said. "If not, all three of us are history."

"We won't even be history," said Dad sadly. "We'll be never-was."

Grandma reached out to Dad to comfort him. Just then something clanged on the floor. I looked down. It was Grandma's Rockettes bracelet. It had fallen off her skinny little-girl wrist. I remembered what Mrs. Coleman-Levin had said about the special powers of the bracelet. Hmmm...

I tried to ask Grandma Leah more about the bracelet and what had happened at the airport. But it was no use. She had lost another year or two. And all she cared about was her birthday.

"Tomorrow's my birthday!" Grandma Leah announced.

"That's right, dear," said Dad.

"How old will I be on my birthday?" asked Grandma Leah.

"I don't know, dear," said Dad. "How old do you think?"

"Seven!" said Grandma Leah.

"Oh, boy," I groaned.

"Or six!" said Grandma Leah. "How old am I now? Five?"

"Dad, this is getting really serious," I said. "What are we going to do?"

"I don't know," said Dad. "But we've got to do something today. Tomorrow may be too late. For all of us."

"Tomorrow's my *birthday*!" Grandma

Leah sang happily. She didn't even seem to remember how upset she was only a moment ago. Or why.

"That's right, dear," said my dad. He patted her on the head.

"I can't help thinking that bracelet of hers has something to do with all of this," I said.

"You could be right," said Dad. "That and the broken metal detector at the airport."

"Exactly," I said. "You know, Mrs. Coleman-Levin said one of the crystals in the bracelet has a strong electromagnetic field. Maybe wearing the bracelet and walking backwards through the broken metal detector was what did this. Maybe Grandma got zapped somehow and that started turning her younger."

"Stranger things have happened," said my dad. "Maybe you are right."

"If I'm right, then our only hope is to get her back in that metal detector as fast as possible. And try to reverse it."

"It's worth a try," said my dad.

"Then we'd better get to the airport now," I said. "There isn't a minute to lose."

Dad got us another cab and told the driver to go straight to LaGuardia. On the way to the airport, Grandma lost another couple of years. She was chattier than ever.

"Tomorrow my *birfday*!" she announced to the cab driver.

"That's nice, little girl," said the driver.

Grandma turned to my dad.

"Am I having a birfday party?" she asked.

"We'll see," said Dad.

"I *want* a birfday party!" she said.

"OK," said Dad. "We'll see what we can do."

"A birfday party with a *cake*," said

Grandma Leah. "And *balloons*. And a *clown*. And *presents*."

"We'll see what we can do," said Dad.

"What presents you buy me for my birfday?" asked Grandma Leah.

"I don't know," said my dad. "What would you like?"

"A pony," said Grandma Leah.

"Well, Mom," said Dad, "I'm not sure we can do that."

My grandma burst into tears.

"I wanna *pony*!" she yelled.

"But, Grandma," I said, "you live in an apartment. How can you keep a pony in an apartment?"

"A *little* pony!" she yelled. "I wanna *little* pony for my 'part-ment!'"

Dad turned to me.

"What can I do here?" he asked.

"Tell her she can have a pony," said the driver.

Chapter 6

"Let me see if I've got this straight," said the head of airport security.

We were sitting in his office at La-Guardia Airport.

"You're telling me that this little girl here is eighty-nine years old," said the man.

"*Tomorrow*!" shouted Grandma Leah. "My eighty-ninth birfday's *tomorrow*! I'm getting a *pony*!"

The man frowned at my grandma on the sofa. Then he continued.

"You're telling me she keeps getting younger and younger. You're telling me that's because she went through a broken metal detector in this airport."

"Right," said my dad.

"You're telling me the only way you can save her life and yours is for her to go back through the broken metal detector. I have to crank it up and make it go backwards. Is that right? Is that what you're asking me to do?"

"You don't have to believe me," said Dad. "Just do it to humor us."

"Airport security does not do things to humor people," said the man.

"Then do it to avoid a big lawsuit," said Dad.

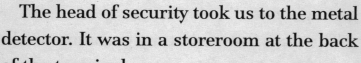

The head of security took us to the metal detector. It was in a storeroom at the back of the terminal.

"All right," he said. "This is the machine she went through the other day."

"The broken one?" said Dad.

"I'm not saying it's broken," said the man. "I'm not saying it's *not* broken. If we let the little girl stand under it, do you promise to go home and leave us alone?"

"We promise," said Dad.

"Fine," said the man. He had all sorts of papers for Dad to sign. I guess that was so we couldn't sue the airport later.

"OK, Grandma," I said, "go and stand in that doorway there."

"No," said my grandma.

"No?" I said. "Why not?"

"I 'fraid," said my grandma.

"Mom, there's nothing to be afraid of," said Dad.

"I 'fraid to go *alone*," said my grandma.

"OK, Grandma," I said, "take my hand. You stand in the doorway, and I'll hold your hand. And here. Hang on to your Rockettes bracelet with the other hand."

Grandma held my hand and her copper bracelet. She stood under the metal detector doorway. I stood on the other side of it.

"Now crank it up in reverse," said my dad.

"There isn't any reverse," said the man.

"Well, then, just do the opposite of what you normally do," said my dad.

The man sighed. He pushed a few switches. He turned a few knobs. I heard a slight humming sound.

Grandma stood under the metal detector, looking maybe two years old. She looked really scared. I felt sorry for her.

At first nothing happened. Then the machine started blipping and blooping and making other strange noises. There was a flash of light and a shower of sparks.

Grandma twitched. And then...she started growing!

"Stay in there, Mom! It's starting to work!" Dad shouted.

Grandma's arms grew longer. And her legs. Pretty soon she looked about five. Grandma stopped crying. She seemed a whole lot happier. The machine kept humming. Soon she was the size of an eight-year-old.

"How are you feeling now, Grandma?" I asked.

"Lots better," she said. She squeezed my hand.

Grandma Leah was growing faster and faster. Now she was a teenager. Her clothes didn't fit her any longer. Dad took his coat and wrapped it around Grandma in the doorway.

Grandma grew older. Now she was nearly

twenty. Now thirty. The machine was speeding up. Now she was forty-five.

"You can stop anytime you like, Mom," said my dad. "Just step out from under the doorway."

Grandma shook her head.

Grandma had hit sixty. Then seventy. She was starting to look like her old self.

"Mom, why not stop now?" said my dad. "You're seventy years old. That's a good age to be."

Grandma Leah shook her head.

"I've already been seventy," she said. "It was a fine age, but I've done that age already. I want to go back to the age I was before all of this nonsense began."

"You mean eighty-eight going on eighty-nine?" I said.

Grandma nodded. Her hair was all gray again. There were wrinkles in her face.

"It's the age I know best," she said. "The age I'm most comfortable with."

Now she was seventy-five. Now eighty. A few seconds later she looked exactly the way she had when she arrived in New York. She stepped out from under the metal detector.

More sparks shot out of the doorway. There was another flash. Then smoke started pouring out of it. The head of airport security grabbed a fire extinguisher and aimed it at the doorway. There was an explosion. Then everything was covered with white foam.

Chapter 7

The Rockettes reunion at Radio City Music Hall was great. Since Grandma Leah hadn't been at the rehearsal, nobody thought she'd be at the performance. Everybody was pumped to see her, and they made a big fuss over her. Grandma loved every minute of it. And we were happy that she was back to normal.

There were a lot of former Rockettes there. Although they were all younger than my grandma, most of them looked way older.

"Leah," they said, "you look so *young*. How in the world do you manage to look so young after all these years?"

Grandma Leah just smiled. Then she looked at Dad and me and smiled some more. She really did seem exactly the same as when she arrived. A little peppier, maybe.

Except there was one small thing. When we took her to the airport for her flight home, Grandma Leah stopped and bought two audio cassettes. One was the New York Philharmonic Orchestra playing Beethoven's Fifth Symphony. The other was Snoop Doggy Dogg.